KNIFEPOINT

A Brace Heller Novel

R. Scott Bolton

Copyright 2019 by R. Scott Bolton
ISBN: 978-0-9997962-2-1
A Rough Edge Studios Production
www.roughedgestudios.com

For Mom, who read the first three chapters of this book ten years before it was finished. Here's how the rest of it goes…

And to the citizens of Ventura County, who endured the disastrous Thomas Fire and the subsequent flooding. #venturastrong

And, once again, thanks to my unmatched panel of proof readers and advice gurus. Their sharp eye for detail and valued suggestions made this book better than it was when I first finished it and, for that, I am eternally grateful. Thanks to Shelley Bolton, Sue Bolton, Doug Bolton, John DeRuvo, Jeff Rogers and Steve Snider.

CHAPTER ONE

There was a guy standing in the hallway in front of my office door. I'd never seen him before but I recognized him instantly and I knew why he was there. It was something in his eyes, a hybrid of sadness and rage, that I'd seen in my business too often before. Whether he'd wind up as a paying client or not remained to be seen, but I knew that customer service leads to referrals and referrals lead to repeat business so I got ready to customer service the shit out of him.

"You Heller?" the man asked as I approached. He wore a pair of khaki slacks and a light blue, button-up shirt, neatly tucked in behind a brown faux leather belt. It was the kind of outfit that was meant to be comfortable and casual, but the tight creases on the sleeves and the slacks told me both had been ironed just that morning.

"That's me," I said, poking the key into the lock and twisting.

"The Shorts and Sandals Detective?"

I bristled. The L.A. Times had done a piece on me last year that I had only agreed to because I thought it'd drum up business. Unfortunately, all it drummed up was a stupid nickname, gleaned from the lousy title of the article: SLEUTHING WITH THE SHORTS AND SANDALS DETECTIVE.

"Yeah," I said. "That's me, too. But I have to tell you I've never been too fond of that nickname."

"Seems like it fits," he said, eyeing me up and down, confirming my t-shirt, cargo shorts and Teva sandals combo.

"I live in California," I said. "Shorts and sandals are kinda the uniform."

"Heard they were gonna make a movie," the man said.

"God, I hope not," I said.

The man fidgeted, embarrassed. "You know, I've been waiting here since seven o'clock."

"Hours are posted." I tapped the little card taped to the back of the window glass. "Eight to five."

"I know," the man said quickly. "I wasn't trying to say you were late. I just wanted you to know I've been waiting."

"Not a problem," I told him. "Come on in." I stood back as he stepped into the tiny waiting room and then followed him inside. He stopped and waited as I stepped past him and opened the door to my office. "Take a seat," I said. "I'd offer you coffee but ... well, there isn't any."

The man sat down in one of the two guest chairs that face my desk. I took the chair behind it. The compact refrigerator in the corner hummed efficiently and I desperately wanted my morning Coke Zero. But it would be unprofessional to drink in front of a new client and, as I recalled, there was only one can in the fridge anyway.

"So," I said. "You know my name ... what's yours?"

"Robert Gleason," the man said. "But please call me Rob."

"All right, Rob. What can I do for you?"

He hesitated, like they all do, wrestling with equal amounts embarrassment, depression and rage. Finally, he choked out the words I knew would be his next: "I think my wife's cheating on me."

"And you'd like me to follow her and find out if that's true or not?"

Another pause. "Yes."

I sat for a moment, musing. Then I said, "Hey. Do you like pancakes?"

"What?"

"Pancakes. You like 'em?"

"Um, sure."

"Let's go get some breakfast," I said. "My treat."

There was a Denny's a couple of miles away so we hopped into my old Toyota Camry and took the beach road. We were silent during the three-minute drive and it wasn't until we were in one of those red vinyl booths—coffee steaming in front of Gleason and a Diet Coke fizzing in front of me—that I asked, "Okay, what makes you think your wife is cheating?"

3

Gleason shook his head. "I don't know," he said. "It's just a feeling."

"You came to a private detective based on a *feeling*?"

"No, it's more than that," Gleason said. "She seems … I don't know … *aloof*. Distant."

"Does she work?" I asked. "Is she busy?"

"Yeah, she runs a doctor's office. She's the office manager," Gleason said. "There's always a lot of paperwork, and Obamacare has only made it worse."

"What about you?"

"At work?"

"Yeah," I said. "Busy?"

"Oh, it's been crazy busy," Gleason said. "I own an auto repair shop here in town and we've been installing catalytic converters left and right. There's been a ring of thieves going around stealing them and we've been overwhelmed with the replacements."

I nodded. "What about at home? Everything good there?"

"Sort of," Gleason said. "I mean, we talk, but we don't go out to dinner or anything."

A server stopped by and quickly and efficiently took our orders. We both asked for buttermilk pancakes. I was thankful Gleason didn't order the Rooty Tooty Fresh 'N Fruity.

"Too tired?" I asked, after the server had sauntered away.

"Sorry?" Gleason asked.

"Too tired," I said. "You know, to go out to dinner or anything."

Gleason nodded. "Yeah, I guess."

"So maybe it's not an affair," I said. "Maybe she's just tired."

"It's not just that," Gleason said. "She's been working late a lot."

"You said she was busy."

"But it seems like it's more now than ever."

"What about you?"

"What about me?"

"Have you been working late?"

"Almost every day," Gleason said. "People are pouring in."

I just looked at him.

"Okay, I get your point," he said after a moment. "But it's not just that."

"How's the sex?" I said.

Gleason was taken aback. After a moment, his face clouded and he said. "None of your business."

"If you want to hire me because you think your wife is having an affair, it *is* my business," I told him. "So, how's the sex?"

He stared at me, and I had the sense he was silently debating whether to answer the question or not. Finally, he said, "It's all right. We don't … do it as often."

"But you do it," I said. "It's just that the frequency is down."

"Yes."

"Because you're tired?"

Gleason sat back and took a deep breath. "Yes," he said. "I guess so."

Our food came, and we dug in. I put a pat of butter between the two pancakes on my plate and then doused them with syrup. Gleason waited until I was finished and then did the same. I took a bite. As good as breakfast gets.

Gleason cut off a little triangle of buttermilk pancake with his fork, stuck it in his mouth and chewed thoughtfully. I don't know if he even tasted it.

"So my point," I said between bites, "Is that maybe you don't need to be running off to a private detective just yet. Maybe you need to start by *talking* to your wife, and then maybe get a little rest. Go on a short vacation, or something, hell, even just a weekend getaway." I ate the last of my bacon, instantly regretting that is was all gone.

Gleason ate another bite of his pancakes and this time I could sense that he was enjoying them. "You may be right," he said. "I may have jumped the gun."

"Maybe," I agreed.

He gave me an odd look. "Forgive me for asking, but do you do this often?"

"Do what?"

"Turn away business?"

I smiled. "No, not too often," I said. "To be honest, cheating wives aren't my favorite type of work. It's boring, it's salacious and it often ends badly, whether there's any cheating going on or not." I took a sip of Diet Coke, the fizz tickling my nose. "That being said, if you get that rest, if you take that small vacation, and you still feel like something's amiss, call me. And I'll do what I do."

I reached into my shirt pocket and took out a business card which I slid across the table. Gleason took it, glanced at it, and tucked it into his wallet. "Thank you," he said.

"And if you feel bad about me turning away business," I said. "You can always buy breakfast. Every little bit helps."

CHAPTER TWO

Playing solitaire on a computer is sterile and asinine. It's all pixels and cursors and about as immersive as a Care Bears movie.

But it was as good a way as any to waste time and, at the moment, I had nothing better to do.

As I clicked and dragged, I thought back to when I was just a kid, maybe eight or nine years old. I remembered lying on the floor at my great grandmother's house in Oxnard, the deck of cards in my left hand, my right hand counting off three at a time. The carpet was shag so the cards didn't lay flat and you couldn't have perfect little stacks there. Instead, the columns kept sliding together, making it more difficult to keep the cards where they were supposed to be and easier to use the mess as an excuse to cheat.

There was no way to cheat playing solitaire on the computer, at least no way that I was aware of. And what would be the point, anyway? It was just another mundane activity to count down the seconds as I waited for the phone to ring or for someone to come through the door and ask for some detecting help. I tried to spice things up by imagining I was in Las Vegas, playing video poker at the bar. But I wasn't playing for real money and there wasn't a server offering me free cocktails so that fantasy died in its tracks.

The mouse danced beneath my fingers and the flashing cursor grabbed an eight of spades and dragged it across to the corresponding pile. A tinny shuffling sound came from the cheap computer speakers. It sounded artificial.

And I guess it was.

I tried to imagine Mickey Spillane's Mike Hammer sitting at a computer, Googling the name of a suspect instead of hunting him down the old-fashioned way, but I couldn't see it. Hammer's porkpie hat just didn't seem right in the glow of an LED screen. Still, I tried to take solace in the fact that Hammer's job and my job were primarily much the same: a lot more waiting and watching than doing.

I pulled the deuce of clubs from the draw pile and digitally slid it over on top of a red three. A few moments later, I dragged the last ace from the pile, placed it at the bottom of a column, and it was all over. I knew this because the cards started cascading down the screen in a kind of psychedelic rainfall pattern.

There was no euphoria on my part. The only emotion was the dread of starting a new game.

I sat back and surveyed the office. Nothing had changed since I started playing solitaire about two hours before. The phone sat smugly on the desk in front of me, content in its silence. The mini-fridge on the table in the corner hummed contentedly, keeping my Cokes and beer at just the right temperature. The coat rack stood in the corner, empty, of course, being more of a novelty item than a practical item here in the warmth of Ventura, California.

The one potential customer I'd had that day had turned out good for one thing: He'd bought me breakfast. Hopefully, he'd go home to his wife tonight, pay her a little more attention, and things would be all right.

If not, he knew where to find me.

I thought about pulling out the checkbook and reviewing my account but decided digital solitaire was far less depressing than an $11.41 bank balance.

My heart leapt as the door to the outside office clicked open and three people came in. I could see their blurry silhouettes through the marbled glass that separated my office from the reception area. More potential clients? This might be a banner day! More likely, though, it was someone selling sandwiches door to door.

Well, I had $11.41. I could afford a sandwich.

At the moment, my receptionist was ... okay, I had no receptionist, so I stood, stepped around from behind the big wooden desk I had purchased at one of the four hundred or so thrift stores in downtown Ventura, and opened the separating door.

There, reaching for the doorknob from the other side, was Johnny Caesar. Two of his bodygoons stood nearby him, one on each side of him like massive, fleshy bookends. Both of them were big-shouldered, big-mustached Mexicans. They gave me the evil eye they reserved specifically for *pinche* gringos. I tried to win them over with my dazzling smile but, alas, to no effect.

The four of us shared a moment of silent, mutual displeasure and then Caesar said, "Heller."

"Caesar," I replied.

Another moment passed. The room temperature seemed to drop a few degrees as the silence dragged on.

"Can we come in?" Caesar finally said.

"*You* can," I told him. "They can stay out here."

The bodygoon on the left started to argue but Caesar cut him off. "Do what he says," he told him, and then pushed past me into the inner office.

"Have some coffee," I told the other two, pointing to the stainless steel pot in the corner. "Have to make it yourselves, though. My receptionist is out today." They glared at me, making those scary faces that kept people from messing with them. I offered them another brilliant show of teeth but, again, they seemed less than impressed.

I closed the door behind me and walked back behind my thrift store desk. Caesar had already taken the clients' chair. I sat, causally checking to make sure the Sig Sauer was in the top right hand drawer and that the top right hand drawer was slightly open. If I needed it, I could get to it.

Caesar and I sat across from each other in silence. He still wore that close-cropped haircut that gave him his street name. "Johnny Caesar" was far more menacing than "Juan Garcia" even if the haircut wasn't menacing at all. Caesar wore a pair of black slacks and a sleeveless, wifebeater-style shirt. A brick-and-black plaid button-up shirt hung loosely over that.

There was something in Caesar's eyes that I hadn't seen before, but I couldn't put my finger on it. Whatever it was, it was something that didn't fit his reputation or his attitude.

A few more moments passed. More silence. I waited patiently. Caesar was the biggest crime lord in Santa Paula, and he and I had a rocky history. Not only were we on opposite sides of the legal fence, we just didn't like one another. Still, I was curious what had brought him the thirty or so miles to my office in downtown Ventura. But I was willing to wait until he was ready to talk.

He shocked the hell out of me when he suddenly began to sob. And then I recognized the out-of-place look in his eyes.

It was vulnerability.

"They killed him," he said between gasping breaths and a shuddering, Herculean effort to stop the tears. "My baby brother. Someone shot him in the head last night and I need to know who done it."

I snatched a Kleenex from the box on the desk (usually reserved for troubled wives who wanted me to catch their cheating husbands in the act) and held it out to him. He didn't take it. I let it drop there on the end of the desk. Only then did Caesar pick it up and dab his eyes. He blew his nose delicately.

"I'm sorry," I told him, and hoped it sounded sincere. It wasn't. Caesar's brother, Diego, was a well-known scumbag. He was the Uday or Qusay Hussein of Santa Paula. His brother was the big cheese and he knew he could get away with murder. And, reportedly, he sometimes did. He had a rap sheet as long as a Columbian python and the reptilian personality to go along with it. Everything from petty theft to aggravated assault had won him jail time and those were just the things he'd been caught at.

The one thing Diego didn't have was his brother's smarts. While Johnny Caesar was the pride of the Garcia family, Diego was the black sheep. He was the younger sibling that wanted everything his older brother had but he didn't have the brains, the talent or the drive to get it. And, because of that, he was bitter and he took that bitterness out on anyone and everyone.

"Tell me what happened," I said.

"Shit, man, don't you read the papers?" Caesar spat. He took a deep heaving breath and finally got his sobbing under control.

I glanced guiltily at the still-rolled Ventura County Post on my desk. I guess maybe there had been something to do other than play solitaire after all. And I hadn't listened to the radio on the way in this morning either. Usually, I would have gotten the local news from the KVTA morning show but this morning I was listening to a CD I'd picked up the night before at a local club. The band was called Slam Alice and I liked what I heard.

But none of that helped me with Johnny Caesar at the moment.

"I haven't had a chance yet, Johnny. Tell me."

"That's the problem. There's not much to tell. Diego ..." His voice broke with the sound of his brother's name. "...Diego was on his way home from Rigoberto's ..."

"The nightclub?"

"Yeah, the nightclub. He always hangs out there on Sundays. Usually gets drunk. Usually gets laid."

"Usually?"

Caesar shot me a glance. "What the fuck difference does that make?"

"I need to know if he was alone, or if he left with somebody."

"Yeah, okay. He was alone when they found him."

"But you don't know if he left with anyone?"

"No. But I can find out."

"It would help. But if you can't, I can."

"I can," Caesar said firmly.

"Go on."

"That's all I know. They found him about halfway between Rigoberto's and his house. You know he lived just a few blocks away?"

I shook my head. I hadn't known that. Was glad I didn't.

"Yeah, just a couple blocks down, off Harvard. He never drove because the cops always put up drunk stops there. They catch a lot of them there."

"What about the cops?" I asked. "They have any leads?"

"Shit," Caesar said, drawing the word out angrily. "They got nothin'. And they aren't gonna bust their balls lookin', either, you know what I mean? Diego was *my* brother, man. They don't give a rat's ass about him."

I couldn't disagree. He was right.

"Anything else you can tell me?"

"Like what?"

"Like did your brother have any enemies that you know of?"

"Shit, man, half of this city is his enemy. A lot of people hated his fucking guts."

There was no denying that, either.

"So, look," Caesar continued. "I know we got a lot of baggage between us, you and me, but I need your help here, Heller. You and me, we got issues, but I know you're a straight-shooter. You're all I got." He was tearing up again and nearly strangling himself to try and stem the flow. After a moment, he lost the struggle. "I need you," he blathered. "It would mean a lot to me." And I knew it was killing him to say so.

15

It wasn't an easy decision. I didn't like Johnny Caesar and I hadn't liked his brother, Diego. As far as I was concerned, Diego's death was simply good riddance. Still, no matter how much I disliked Caesar, he was a powerful and important part of the local crime scene. It wouldn't hurt to have him owe me a favor. There was no question that, someday, I'd have to ask him for one.

"Yeah, I'll help you," I told him. It felt wrong to say it but sometimes you have to deal with the devil. "On two conditions."

Caesar actually managed a weak smile of gratitude. "Okay."

"One: I find out who did this we go to the police first. They choose to ignore us, you do what you have to do, but I want them to have first crack."

Caesar froze for a moment, and then reluctantly nodded.

"Two: I do this alone. I don't want any of your boys following me, checking up on me. It cramps my style and it scares witnesses."

"You got it," Caesar told me. "I give my word."

"Two hundred a day," I continued, "Plus expenses. Five hundred dollar retainer up front."

I thought Caesar might blanch, but instead he stood up, pulled a wallet out of his back pocket (it was attached to a belt loop with a long silver chain and bore a bright green marijuana leaf on its side) and counted out five one-hundred dollar bills from a stack that looked a half-inch thick.

"You find out who did this," Caesar said strongly, making it sound like an order. He stuffed his wallet back into his pants.

I gathered the money off of the desktop and stacked it neatly.

"That's what you're paying me for," I told him.

CHAPTER THREE

As unhappy as I was to find myself on Johnny Caesar's payroll, I knew there was one other person would be even less happy: Marina. We were on our way downtown for the evening, chatting about our work days, when I told her about my morning meeting.

"So he wants me to find out who killed his brother," I said.

Marina actually laughed. "I would have loved to have seen his face when you told him to go to hell."

"Yeah, well, I didn't," I said. "I told him I would."

There was about three seconds of complete, deadly silence. And then Marina exploded. "Are you out of your fucking mind? Why would you help *him?*"

She glared at me with angry disgust, like I was a species of cockroach she had never seen before, as I took the California Street exit off the 101 Freeway.

"Why?" Marina demanded. "Don't you know what he's done? What he's capable of?"

"Of course, I do," I said "But ...."

"I know. I've seen it firsthand."

And she had, of course. Many of Marina's social work clients in Santa Paula were victims of Johnny Caesar, either directly or indirectly, and owed him their current woes. One of them was an ex-hooker with a six-inch slash ribboned across her face and a severed Achilles tendon that left her in wheel chair. She'd taken money given to her for a backseat blowjob and used it to buy a burrito and a chocolate malt at Foster's Freeze. When one of Caesar's enforcers saw her there when she should have been working, he informed Johnny.

Caesar told him to do what an enforcer does. Penny-wise, pound-foolish.

My lips parted as I again tried to explain myself and I realized Marina's mind wasn't about to be changed. And I could understand why. But I couldn't renege on a deal already agreed to, especially with someone like Johnny Caesar, and it had nothing to do with my bank account sitting now at over four hundred dollars instead of less than twelve. (I had kept out a hundred for the club tonight).

I took California Street past my office to Main, turned left and drove a couple blocks past South Oak. I was lucky enough to find an open parking place near the bar, pulled Marina's Miata into the place, levered the emergency brake and killed the engine. The thump of live rock'n'roll throbbed through the floorboards.

We sat for a few moments in pregnant silence.

"I'm not mad at you," Marina said after a moment. "I'm mad at the situation."

"I know."

"Johnny Caesar is a fucking scumbag," Marina continued. "But I can see the benefit of your offering to help him."

"It's not like I'm doing it for free."

"That really doesn't matter."

"Yes, it does. It's not the money, it's the arrangement. If Caesar wants me to work for him, he pays me like any other client. The favor isn't the work; the favor is accepting the work."

"I understand that. Even if he's paying you, he'll still owe you a favor."

"Just because I took the work. He knows I wouldn't have otherwise."

"Does he?"

"He does."

Marina took a deep breath and let it out slowly. "But I don't have to like it."

"No, you don't. I don't like it much myself."

Marina licked her lips thoughtfully and nodded once. Her fingers touched the door handle and then hung there.

"And I guess someone did murder his brother," she said. "You can't just let them get away with that."

"Probably not," I said.

We fed the meter and crossed the sidewalk to the entrance of the Star Lounge. The place wasn't exactly full, but it was busy enough, with only a few seats available at the bar and both pool tables sporting a line of quarters that reserved the next few games.

KNIFEPOINT

Marina's long black hair, black spaghetti-strapped top and tight blue jeans drew a few lascivious glances and I certainly understood why. Sadly, my black jeans and Black Sabbath t-shirt didn't have quite the same effect.

The bartender, Jeanette, looked up from the Bud Light she was drawing, caught sight of Marina and me, and fluttered her fingers in a friendly wave. It wasn't long after we took two of the remaining barstools that she was back in front of us, setting a martini glass with yellow liquid in front of Marina and a high ball glass half-filled with brown liquid in front of me. I took an appreciative sip. Makers Mark. Life is good.

A band was on stage playing the sort of pop punk that is completely indistinguishable from one band to another. Despite their undeniable onstage energy, I wasn't interested. The other people in the bar weren't much interested either. Some sat at tables and watched the band through alcohol-glazed eyes. Others carried on loud conversations as though the band wasn't there at all. The rest were obviously with the band, worshiping them like they were the reincarnation of the Ramones or something.

Which they weren't.

I gulped down the rest of my whiskey and felt instant remorse. Makers Mark should be sipped and savored, not shot. But sometimes, you just need to throw it back. The sudden oak burn felt good as it traced its way down to my stomach. I looked in Jeanette's direction and watched as she mixed up a rum and Coke. As always, she wore spiked heels, tight black slacks and a solid white tank top that exposed far too much of her alluring cleavage, especially when she leaned over to wash a glass or scoop up some ice. That was by design, of course. Modern science has proven that the ratio of exposed cleavage increases tip giving exponentially. And it seemed to be working judging from the wad of bills the rum and Coke guy gave her. Jeanette rang up the sale and glanced at me. I wiggled my empty glass and she gave that bright smile of hers, grabbed the familiar shape of the wax-topped Markers Mark bottle and filled me back up.

The band was too loud to talk over without screaming so we just sat there for a while and watched. Because the stage was located to the right and in front of the bar, I had to sit on the stool with my back to Jeanette. Marina faced the bar, watching the band in the spotted mirror behind the wall of bottles. Out of the corner of my eye I saw her drain her glass and signal for another.

Finishing with a song that their loyal followers seemed ready to sacrifice themselves to, the band finally ended their set and started tearing down. Jeanette returned and swapped Marina's empty martini glass with a full one. Marina took a sip, gave a pleased smile.

"It doesn't matter if they used the cheapest booze they can find," she said. "But, damn, these are good lemon drops."

"Jeanette's a master."

"Yes, she is."

I drank a little more whiskey. I sipped. I savored. I did so carefully, making up for my past indiscretion.

Marina looked into the mirror behind the bar. "Your boys are here," she said, nodding over her shoulder.

I followed her nod to the door where a quartet of long-haired twenty-somethings were filing in, arms loaded with musical instruments and accessories. WEAPONS GRADE CHARM was stenciled across most of the items in white spray paint. They took about fifteen minutes to set up, grab a few beers and start their set.

I ordered a Diet Coke before the band began playing and drank it with a straw as the band went through their motions. I had seen them live at the Red Cove a few nights ago and I was impressed with their performance and attitude. This was a band I could dedicate myself to, a band I believed in.

The audience swelled to about fifteen while WGC played and they all seemed to enjoy the show, some of them putting down their pool cues to get into the rock'n'roll. Afterwards, I invited the band over to the bar, introduced them to Marina, bought them all drinks, and we talked about the possibility of my managing the band. They seemed very open to it.

At first, they always do. Ah, the wide-eyed innocence of youth.

CHAPTER FOUR

The fiery orb of the sun burned through my bedroom window when I awoke the next morning and the heat coming through the glass pane was enough to make laying around waiting for the alarm to go off uncomfortable. So I cancelled the alarm, threw off the blankets and padded to the bathroom. Wurzel didn't budge, laying on his back, legs in the air, eyes closed in sleepy doggy bliss as the solar rays soaked into his black and white fur. I had to stop for a moment and watch to make sure he was breathing. He was.

Marina had left at about two in the morning but had taken the time to silently make up her side of the bed. The cuteness of it all forced me to smile and feel a warm burst of love for her. It was Tuesday, a work day, and she liked to wake up at home. Otherwise, she said, her entire day was screwed up. It seemed to me that getting up and driving home at two in the morning was what would screw up your day.

Freshly showered, I threw on a pair of blue jeans, a black t-shirt and my cheap ass WalMart sneakers. I tucked the Sig Sauer and its Scout rig as comfortably as possible into the front of my pants.

KNIFEPOINT

Outside, I stood on the street for a couple of minutes deciding whether to take the Camaro or the Camry. The Camaro was flashier and more fun to drive but that was the problem. Everybody noticed it. Nobody noticed the Camry. It was old and beige and boring. So I swung open its creaky door, tossed the gun and its holster on the passenger's seat and dropped in. A few minutes later, I was on the 126 heading toward Santa Paula.

I took the Palm Avenue off-ramp and stopped off at the McDonald's there for a bacon cheese biscuit and a Diet Coke. I ate as I drove up Harvard toward Fillmore, mentally calculating the extra gym time I'd have to put in to work off breakfast. It wasn't pretty.

The parking lot at La Cabana restaurant was empty but I expected it to be at that time of the morning. My plan was to walk Diego Garcia's final path just to get a feel for where everything had gone down. By the time I was done, if I was lucky, La Cabana would be open for lunch. An 18C combo and a jumbo turbo margarita sounded pretty good, even though I'd just eaten breakfast. More gym time, but it would be worth it.

The sun moved slowly toward its zenith and the temperature was already rising as I started down Harvard. I wanted to remove my sports coat but couldn't because the holster with the Sig Sauer was beneath it and I didn't want to frighten the locals. Not that, in this neighborhood, I would have frightened many.

I walked west past Rigoberto's, where Diego had

swallowed his last cocktail (closed until this evening). I passed quaint homes with lawns either manicured or unkempt, a couple more Mexican food restaurants (one apparently specializing in seafood) and a liquor store. I stopped at the liquor store and bought a lottery ticket. I scratched it off in the parking lot and then tossed the worthless ticket in a battered trashcan there. Let someone else enter it in the Second Chance drawing. I still felt all right about it. After all, it's for our schools.

Finally, I came to the barren lot where Diego's body had been found. It was just a square of undeveloped land; maybe a house had stood there at one time or a business of some sort. But now it was just dirt and weeds. The weeds were tall near the back of the lot but many had been trampled closer to the street by the feet of police detectives and investigators who had worked at the scene. There was no chalk outline where Diego had been found but it wasn't hard to figure out where he had fallen. A sticky splash of blood that looked a little like an oil spill in a crop circle marked the spot. I was always surprised that gore like that didn't get cleaned up even though I knew that was usually the case.

I wandered around the lot awhile, peeking behind rocks and scuffing my feet through the thicker weeds, hoping to kick something heavier than a small stone ... something, say, the size of a murder weapon. I was sure the cops had been through it all already but better safe than sorry. Johnny Caesar had been right—his brother's murder wouldn't be at the top of the local police investigation list and it was possible something had been overlooked. An hour of shuffling and peeking and I was convinced there was nothing to be found.

I sat on a large rock for a moment and observed the lot. Diego had probably been shot from either the street or the sidewalk judging from the pattern of the blood-stained dirt. Although no one had wanted to clean it up, no one wanted to tread on wet blood either and it was fairly undisturbed. Could it have been just a simple drive-by? Diego's unlucky day? Maybe. But it probably wasn't an official gang hit. Taking out Johnny Caesar's brother was an act of war and there was no one in Santa Paula that I was aware of that was anywhere near as powerful as Johnny. An act like that would be plain suicide. More likely was that Diego was just in the wrong place at the wrong time. Maybe someone had tried to rob him or maybe some green-behind-the-ears gang member was trying to earn Brownie points by taking out a rival never even realizing that he'd killed Johnny Caesar's brother. If that was the case, I almost felt sorry for the poor schlub. What was left of his short life would be nothing less than a living hell. I was reminded of a line from *Pulp Fiction*: Johnny would get Medieval on their ass.

If this was just a random shooting, I thought, *this just got a whole lot more difficult.*

My pant legs were infested with foxtails and floured with dust. Not for the first time, I wished I was wearing the shorts promised in that "Shorts and Sandals" article in the L.A. Times. I brushed some of the dust off but the foxtails weren't so willing to go. I sat on my rock and began picking them out. There were a lot of them. It was going to take some time.

I had nearly finished the first pant leg when a shadow passed over me. I looked up.

There were five of them and I should have heard them coming. They were Hispanic and two of them were monstrous, standing over six feet and sporting huge shoulders. Another was thin but well-muscled and was shirtless to show off his build and his tattoos. The other two were slight and rail thin.

They all wore their clothing loosely, but I could tell that at least two of them were carrying.

"Hi," I said cheerily. "How do you think Heloise would recommend getting these stickers out?"

One of the big guys smirked but didn't laugh. He wore a red plaid shirt over a white t-shirt, a black skullcap and dark sunglasses. The others obviously had no idea who Heloise was.

The smallest guy in the group suddenly stepped forward, his chest thrust out angrily, his mouth drawing into a ferocious frown.

It was always the little guy.

He thrust a bony finger at me. "The fuck you think you're doing here, man?" He was the only one not wearing sunglasses and I could see that his eyes were wide and a little wild. A tiny vein pulsed in the center of his forehead. There was a name for his affliction: Small Man's Syndrome.

I pinched a foxtail and flicked it away. "I'm a Starbucks scout and we're looking for a new location," I told him. "What do you guys think? You like a good Espresso Macchiato?"

The thin guy looked like he'd been slapped. He wasn't used to people talking to him that way, especially when his posse was standing behind him. "You fucking with me, man?" His finger still pointed at me but now it was shaking a little. "You don't want to be fucking with me." He said "fucking" like "fuckeen."

"Of course I'm fucking with you," I told him. I stood up so that he had to look up at me when he talked. I was big, but I still felt dwarfed by the two beefy guys in the back. They were each at least an inch taller than me and probably had forty pounds on me each. Thankfully, they also looked a little soft.

I focused my attention on the small guy. "Here's what I'm doing," I said. "I'm sitting here minding my own business. Which means, actually, that you're the one fucking with *me*."

I might as well have spit in his face. "Hey, man, we'll kick your fucking ass!" he said. "We'll fucking kill you, *gringo!*" He scrabbled for the bulge at his waist where he had no doubt stashed his gun.

"I guess maybe a Starbuck's isn't such a good idea," I

said. Then I drove the palm of my hand into the small guy's nose. There was a splash of warm blood on my fingers and he went down like a marionette whose strings had been cut. I jabbed my elbow into the side of the shirtless guy's head to the right of me and felt, rather than saw, him go down, too.

I guessed the big guys would be the slowest to react and, so far, I was right. The third little guy jumped on my back but, seeing as he weighed about eight pounds, I just threw him off, giving him a little arc so he'd hit the ground hard. He *oofed* as the impact knocked the wind out of him.

One of the big guys grabbed my arm and I rolled my shoulder and shrugged him off. Caught off guard, his momentum continued to carry him forward and I used his own energy to put more force into a straight jab with my left fist. He grunted, wobbled and stumbled back, but I knew I hadn't done any real damage. A rock underfoot caught his heel, however, and he crashed to the ground.

The second big guy snatched for the gun in the front of his pants. I grabbed his hands through the material of his unbuttoned shirt and twisted them around until they were tied up in the cloth. Then I jabbed my forehead into his nose and wedged my foot beneath his heel, driving him backward. He went down like King Kong off the Empire State Building.

As the five of them tried to shake off the surprise assault and get their feet back under them, I did what anyone should do when they're involved in a five against one fight.

I ran.

CHAPTER FIVE

When I got back to La Cabana, sweaty and gasping for breath, there was no sign of my five new friends. I had either shaken them or they had decided I wasn't worth pursuing. That was a good thing. I was sick of running in the early afternoon heat.

There were several cars in the parking lot now and, as I hoped, La Cabana was open for lunch. I went in through the outside patio and took a seat at the bar. There were still a few foxtails in my pant legs and they scratched at my skin like hungry little insects.

The bartender was apparently off delivering drinks so the bar area was virtually empty except for the hulking Hispanic man sitting beside me. It was Puño, of course, and I wasn't surprised to see him. He was probably the reason there was no one else in the bar. He had a way of scaring everyone away.

Puño's huge brown shoulders bulged out of his Harley-Davidson tank top and his enormous biceps rippled as he rubbed the bristly stubble on his jaw. His long black hair cascaded about midway down his back and he wore a pair of sunglasses that looked like they'd come from some bad Japanese monster movie. A single earring dangled from his left ear ... a thin silver chain from which hung a tiny chrome skull. A solitary shot glass was on the bar before him and beside it was a half-empty bottle of Patron tequila.

I reached over and slid the shot glass closer to me, then took the bottle of Patron and poured a short shot. It was too early to be drinking straight up, but it had been a rough morning. The warm trickle down my throat made the world just a little better.

"How goes the rock'n'roll business?" Puño asked, without looking up from the bar.

"Got a new act, I think," I said. "Weapons Grade Charm. I think they'll sign this week."

"They real music or that jungle crap you listen to?"

"You travel the world following mariachi festivals and yet my music is jungle crap?"

"Mariachi is an art form."

"So is Black Sabbath."

"*Were*," Puno said.

"Touché'" I replied.

We were quiet a moment. Sipping.

"So where were you when your fellow gang bangers tried to kick my ass?" I asked.

"The *problema* with gangs is, I wouldn't want to be a member of any gang that would have me as a member." He took the bottle and the shot glass back, refilled, and drank.

"Doesn't answer the question," I said. "Where were

33

you?"

"Close enough to see you run," Puño said. "Sissy."

"Sissy? Did you say 'sissy?' You realize that's considered insensitive these days."

"Woulda used another word," he said, "But there's a lady present."

At that moment, Sylvia turned the corner with a basket of tortilla chips and a bowl of salsa in her hand. Her dark brown eyes brightened when she saw me. They always do.

"Hi, Brace! Puño said you were coming." She set the chips and salsa in front of him. "Can I get you a margarita?"

"You can," I said. "Jumbo turbo."

"Rocks, right?"

"Of course."

"Anything to eat?"

"18c."

"You got it."

She went to work on the margarita. I went to work on the chips and salsa. They weren't as good as they used to be when they made them fresh here, but they served their purpose. Puño continued working on the Patron.

"Don't know why you waste good tequila," Puño said, "By mixing it with lemonade."

"It's not lemonade." I said. "And they don't use Patron in the margaritas."

"Then what's the point?" He took another sip of

KNIFEPOINT

Patron.

I thought about that for a moment. "Maybe you're right." I said, and ate another brittle chip. "So you know any of those guys? My friends at the lot back there?"

"Know 'em all," Puño said. "Belong to small, wanna-be gang on the other side of town."

"What are they doing out this way? Not very smart for them to be hanging out where Johnny Caesar's brother was gunned down."

"No. Not very."

"Might make someone think they had something to do with it."

"They didn't," Puño said. "They're stupid but they're not that stupid. So what'd you do to piss them off?"

"Tried to open a Starbucks."

"You *gringos* and your Starbucks," Puño smirked.

"Here's some news," I said. "I'm working for Johnny Caesar. Looking into who killed his brother."

Puño's hand stopped halfway to his mouth. The tequila sloshed in the glass but he didn't spill a drop. "You think that's smart?"

"Maybe. Maybe not. He asked me to do it as a favor. I figured I might be able to use a favor from him in the future."

"Like you can trust him to return the favor."

"There is that," I admitted.

"Sounds risky," Puño said.

"Might be. Too late to back out now."

"Yep."

Sylvia brought me my margarita. I smiled at her with all the love I hold for those who bring me margaritas. I took a sip. As usual, it was wonderful, inferior tequila or not.

"So what are *you* doing out here?" I asked Puño.

"On my way to Oxnard," he said. "Saw your car. Figured I'd stick around, see what's up. Knew you'd end up here eventually."

"What's in Oxnard?"

Puño drained the rest of his Patron. "Stuff," he said. He stood and grabbed his leather jacket off the chair beside him. It was far too warm to wear leather, but that's not why he had it. I could see the stiff form beneath that was either a shotgun or a cattle prod. I didn't ask which.

"Good luck," Puño told me. "You're gonna need it."

"Why do I need luck," I asked him, "when I've got you?"

He shrugged into his coat and walked out. A minute later, Sylvia came back with my 18c. Two enchilada combo, one ground beef, the other shredded, plus rice and beans. I took another sip of my margarita and thanked her.

For the moment, all seemed right with the world.

CHAPTER SIX

"So who is it this time? The Evil Weevils? Bacon and the Bits? Green Jelly?"

I was back in my office and on the phone with my attorney, Bob Kaplan. Bob had represented me for nearly five years despite the fact he did not share my taste in music. He had left a message on my office machine, returning my call. The other message was from Johnny Caesar, who wanted an update. He wouldn't be getting one today.

"There was already a band called Green Jelly," I told Bob. "Used to be Green Jello until they got sued."

"Really? No shit."

"No shit. Figured you'd know that, being a big city attorney and all."

"Can't know everything," Bob said. "Kill the thrill of discovery."

The window was open and I could hear the afternoon traffic on California Street starting to build up to rush hour speed. The sharp smell of auto exhaust overcame the sweet fragrance of ocean air. It was my least favorite time of day.

"These guys are called *Weapons Grade Charm*, and

they're pretty good."

"What kind of music?"

"Classic hard rock," I said. "Heavier than KISS, but nowhere as extreme as, say, Slipknot."

"You ever going to find someone who's actually relevant to today's music scene?"

"I hate when people use that word when referring to music," I said. "Music is music. It shouldn't be relevant."

"If you say so," Bob said. "You promise them an advance?"

I thought about the $400 in my checking account. "No. They agreed to move forward without one."

"Okay, I'll write up an agreement. What's your game plan?"

"Tommy Hogart's playing the Ventura Theater in a couple months," I said. "I'm gonna pull some strings and see if I can't get them to open for him."

"Hogart big?"

"He'll fill the place easily. And I think he and my guys are a good match."

"Sounds good," Bob said. "I'll e-mail you the agreement later."

"Thanks, Bob."

"Later."

I dropped the phone in the cradle and leaned back in my office chair. It creaked ominously. I put my heels on the desktop and my hands behind my head and thought about stuff. There wasn't much to think about. Bob was

handling the *Weapons Grade Charm* management agreement, I knew nothing more about who had killed Johnny
Caesar's brother, and five guys had tried to beat me up
for threatening to open a Starbuck's.

Not a very productive day.

The phone rang. I let it ring a few times, to give the
caller the impression I was busy, and then picked it up.
"Heller Investigations."

"Hey. Whatcha doin'?" It was Marina, calling from
her office in Santa Paula.

"Just sitting around, thinkin'" I told her.

"Well, don't hurt yourself."

"Funny."

"Meet you at the gym?"

I frowned. "Yeah," I said reluctantly. "Gotta work off
lunch."

"What'd you have?"

"18c and a jumbo margarita."

"Oh, yeah," Marina said. "You're gonna have to work
hard. See you in about half an hour?"

"I'll be there."

I hung up, turned off the computer screen, hit the
lights and headed out.

CHAPTER SEVEN

It was difficult to keep my mind focused on jogging with Marina bouncing delightfully alongside me. A completely different form of exercise kept popping into my head. We ran along on side-by-side treadmills, me starting to glisten with the first signs of perspiration and Marina still looking as fresh as the proverbial daisy. I wore a pair of worn sneakers, an equally worn pair of grey sweatpants and an ancient Motorhead t-shirt that had once been black but after years of being washed was now a dusty charcoal. Marina was in light blue leggings and a matching mesh center bra top she bought online from Fila. Her running shoes were as bright and as white as they day she'd bought them and I knew that was months ago.

Why she insisted on being stylish when exercising was beyond me. But it worked for her.

Come to think of it, it worked for me, too.

Marina touched a control on the front of her treadmill and it sped up minutely. "So you don't think the guys who beat you up had anything to do with Diego's death?"

"First, and let's be clear about this, they didn't beat me up," I said. "And, second, no, I don't."

"Why not?"

"Because Puño said they didn't."

"And that's good enough for you?"

"Good enough for me."

"So what were they doing there, then?"

"Could be anything. They wanted to see the crime scene. They wanted to look for blood. They were out for a walk. They saw a white guy poking around their neighborhood and thought maybe he needed directions. Could be anything."

"But they're not your guys."

"I don't think so."

"Because Puño doesn't think so."

"That's the main reason. The other is that it doesn't make sense. If they were the guys who killed Diego, showing up there would be like signing their death warrant."

"So where do you go from here?"

"Gonna go see Andy at the paper tomorrow," I said. "And then I'll call Powell and see what he knows. If anything."

"Why didn't you start there?" Marina asked. "Seems like Powell would know more than the newspaper, being a police detective and all."

"He might," I said. "But he also might have some kind of theory that will taint his thinking process. Not his fault; happens to the best of us. But I want to have a clear line of thinking when I go see him."

"You trust Puño more than a police detective?"

"I'm not saying that. I'm just saying that Steve's job is to take an unsolved crime and solve it. In order to do that, he has to follow his usual path of thinking and that might take him the wrong way. I want to have my own sense of direction before I start following his."

"His path might also be the right one."

"That's true. But I'd rather get there in my own way than follow someone else's lead."

"Ah, the male ego."

"It's got nothing to do with ego," I said. "I just don't want anyone else's theory ...and that's all we've got at the moment, is theories ... clouding my own."

Marina mused on this for a moment and then said, "I see."

We finished our run and turned off the treadmills. There was a white plastic bench nearby and we took our towels with us and sat on it. Marina blotted the minuscule drops of sweat from her upper lip and was done. By the time I finished wiping down my hands, arm and face, my towel was sopping.

"So, what's for dinner?" I asked.

"What do you feel like?" Marina said.

"I dunno. What do you feel like?"

"I dunno."

And so it went until we wound up at Carl's Jr. eating burgers and fries with the rest of the urban peasants.

Which meant we'd be back at the gym tomorrow, working off our Famous Stars.

CHAPTER EIGHT

It's never good news when the phone rings at three in the morning. It's never the Lottery Commission calling to tell you that you just hit all six numbers *and* the Mega. It's never Steven Spielberg calling to option your life story for his next film. And it's never, ever Salma Hayek calling to say she's decided that she can't live without you.

No. It's never good news. It's always bad.

So when the phone rang and I peeled my eyes open and found a glowing red 3:03 staring back at me from the alarm clock on the nightstand, I knew the news wasn't good. I just didn't know who was calling with bad news until I heard Kristyn's voice on the other end.

"Brace?"

"Krisytn? You all right?"

"Yes." Her voice was a frightened whisper. "No, I ... He's still here, Brace."

Kristyn was a bartender over at O'Leary's near the government center. According to Marina she made the best Washington Apple martinis in town.

I looked over at Marina's side of the bed. It was empty and neatly made up. Wurzel lay near the pillow, snoring softly.

"Where?" I asked.

"He's waiting outside, in his car."

"Where are you?"

"Inside. At the bar."

"Door locked?"

"Yes."

"Stay there. Don't let him see you. I'll be there in ten minutes."

"Thanks, Brace."

I was there in seven minutes, wearing only my sleep sweats, an oversized black t-shirt and my slippers. I didn't even bother strapping on the Sig Sauer but instead carried it in its holster by hand.

When I drove up there were only two cars in the parking lot: Kristyn's Volkswagen Cabriolet and a boat-like Cadillac Fleetwood at least two decades old. It was too dark to see if there was anybody inside the Caddy, but I cruised by close enough to casually memorize the license plate, then parked near the bar's front door, killed the lights and stepped out of the Camaro.

Almost immediately, the big Cadillac engine roared to life and the sedan tore out of the parking lot, its tires screeching in protest. I watched it disappear, its bright red taillights fading into the early morning fog, and then took the three steps up that led to the glass door.

I could see Kristyn behind the bar near the back and she jumped a little when I knocked on the glass. Her startled look turned to one of blessed relief when she recognized me.

She opened the door and stepped back to let me in. She quickly locked the door behind me. Smart girl.

"You okay?" I knew the answer before she answered. She was pale and jittery.

"Yeah," she fibbed. "Thanks for coming out, Brace."

I took a seat on one of the tall stools and Kristyn slipped behind the bar. She poured a glass of Kahlua Especial on the rocks and slid it over. I took a sip. It was a good drink for three in the morning.

"I'm glad you called," I said. "Tell me about this guy again."

"He's been coming in about three nights a week or so for about a month now," she said. "I didn't pay much attention to him at first but, after a while ... well, you know. People start to become regulars."

I knew. I was a regular at about half the bars in Ventura.

"And we got friendly. He would come in, sit where I could wait on him, and we'd talk. About two weeks ago, he asked me out."

"And that's when you told him no, and he got pissed off, threw his drink on the floor and stormed out of here."

"Right. That's when I first called you, because it scared me."

"So when did he start coming back?"

"Last week. At first he sat at a table instead of at the

bar and I thought everything was going to be cool. Then, he came back to the bar. Sarah knew that he and I had issues—you know, Sarah, right?—and she always tried to take him for me. A couple of days ago, though, I was here alone and I had to serve him. When I asked him what he wanted to drink, he called me a fucking whore and walked out again."

"And he kisses his mama with that mouth?"

Kristyn smiled and the corners of her impossibly blue eyes crinkled engagingly when she did. "Since then, he just sits at the bar and glares at me. When I ask him what he'd like, he just stares and doesn't answer. It's scary, you know? That's why when I saw his car outside tonight, and I was closing by myself, I didn't want to go out there."

"That was smart. Has he ever followed you home?"

"I don't think so. Not that I know of. I usually go home pretty late and I think I would have seen somebody following me."

"Good. What's this guy's name?"

"Ian. Ian Kilgore. I've got a credit card receipt if that will help you find him."

"Not anymore," I said. "They don't put the entire card number on the receipt so it's no help."

"That's right."

"I don't need it anyway. I got his license plate. I'll track him down tomorrow." I had another sip of Kahlua and was shocked to discover I had nearly drained it. "You ready to get out of here?"

"Yeah. Just let me get my coat."

Kristyn went into the back and came out a moment later with a pink sweatshirt. As she slipped into it, I drained the last of the melted ice in my glass. There was still a hint of coffee flavor in it. Kristyn took the glass from me, dumped out the ice and rinsed the glass. We headed for the door.

"Don't go straight home," I told her. "Drive around for a while. I'll follow right behind. That way if Mr. Kilgore is out there somewhere and decides to do something stupid, it'll give me time to spot him."

"Okay."

We stepped into the misty night air and I took a deep breath, savoring the salty scent that had blown in from the sea. Another reason to love Ventura. Kristyn locked the door with a key that hung with its many brethren on a ring attached to a pink rabbit foot. Maybe Kilgore was an animal lover and was angry with Kristyn for her keyring.

"Thanks again, Brace," Kristyn said, stepping on her tiptoes and giving me a quick peck on the cheek. Those not as tough as me might have blushed. "Tell Marina I said hello."

"I will. Now go home. Get some sleep," I told her.

She walked out to her Cabriolet and I waited by the Camaro until she got in and got the engine warmed up. She drove around town for a little while and I followed her clandestinely but carefully. No one else was with us. No one else was out at all, it seemed. After about twenty minutes, she drove up to her apartment at Todd Ranch, gave me a little wave and disappeared inside. I watched and listened carefully for a moment, and then headed back home.

CHAPTER NINE

I was on the road, heading toward the offices of the Ventura County Post. The rising sun slanted down and slowly burned the morning dew off the windows of the Camry. Tom Spence was on the radio, talking with his newsman Rich about a new production over at the Flying H Theater. Marina and I already had tickets. She enjoyed live theater and the Flying H was famous for quality performances.

As I drove, I puzzled over a few important items. One: Who had reason to kill Johnny Caesar's brother? Two: Who had the *balls* to kill Johnny Caesar's brother? And three: Was *Weapons Grade Charm* the band that was going to make a name for me? These were questions that I would have liked answers to, but they were not immediately forthcoming.

I stopped at the Jack in the Box on Victoria Avenue and bought two Sourdough Breakfast Sandwiches and two large Diet Cokes, then took the frontage road that paralleled the freeway toward the Post. I drove past a Harley-Davidson shop, Golf N'Stuff, a membership gym and a Coca-Cola plant. The aging shock absorbers of the Camry groaned as I bounded up the driveway to the parking lot.

Andy Larsen was the managing editor of the Post and he and I had all but grown up together. We first met decades ago when I worked at the Mann Theatres in the Esplanade shopping center. I was a lowly usher; Andy was the film critic for the local free paper, the Ventura County Reporter. Our tastes and obsessions in movies were similar and we quickly became friends. Both of us had grown in the twenty or so years since then: Andy had gone from the film critic of the weekly Reporter to the managing editor of the daily Post and I had become the sexy, brilliant and universally respected detective that I was today.

Andy had come a lot further.

When I entered his office, Andy was sitting at his desk, his feet up on the blotter, a phone pressed to his ear. The chair he was lounging in groaned with the stress of his 350 pound girth. His bald head gleamed under the fluorescent lighting except where a wreath of jumbled gray hair surrounded it. There were uneven stacks of paper reaching up all around him like crumbling Roman columns—it looked as though someone had simply opened the door and thrown handfuls of the stuff in there—but I knew that Andy could tell you exactly what was on every sheet and exactly where he could find it.

You know the saying: A clean desk is the sign of a sick mind. If that was true, Andy had the healthiest mind of anyone I knew.

KNIFEPOINT

I put one of the Diet Cokes on the desk in front of Andy and a sandwich beside it. Andy nodded a greeting and I sat down, unwrapped my sandwich and took a bite.

"Get it to me by noon," Andy said into the receiver, "And I'll try to get it in tomorrow. No promises, though. Okay? Thanks." He dropped the receiver into its cradle and reached for the sandwich. "Great," he said to me. "Just what I needed. More red meat." He took a bite and almost half the sandwich disappeared.

"You're welcome," I told him. "What's going on?"

"No, seriously, man, thanks. I can feel my arteries hardening as we speak." He took another mammoth bite, washed it down with a swig of soda, and made a face. "Diet?"

"Of course. I know you're watching your weight."

"Fuck you." A third bite and the sandwich was gone. He crumpled the greasy wrapper and threw it flawlessly into the overflowing wastebasket where it joined dozens of other depleted fast food wrappers. "What are you doing here anyway?"

"I need some information."

"Of course. Only time you come by these days."

"That and when I need a movie rental." Andy was still the paper's film critic and got a dozen new DVDs in the mail each week.

"That's true." He took another suck on the soda straw. "What do you need?"

"I need anything you can give me on Diego Garcia."

"You know he's dead, right? No point in chasing him down now."

"I need to find out who killed him."

"Who cares? The town's light one scumbag. We're better off."

"I don't disagree," I said. "But his brother's paying me to find out."

Andy raised his eyebrow. "You're working for Johnny Caesar? Jesus, talk about strange bedfellows. What? He paying you a fortune?"

"Standard rate. I'm doing this for the favor aspect."

Andy nodded. "Your business, you can probably use a favor from a guy like that." He fished a notepad from beneath the sea of paper on his desk and scribbled a quick note. "What, exactly, are you looking for?"

"Anything and everything. You know how it works. I'll throw it all against a wall and see what sticks."

"I'll tell you this," Andy said. "There won't be any good news. They don't make 'em much worse than Diego Garcia." He took another sip of soda. "Give me a day or two."

"I appreciate it, Andy."

"Yeah. Blow me."

"You wish."

Like I said, we'd been friends for a long time.

CHAPTER TEN

Somewhere, I'd picked up a tail.

I first realized I was being followed when the driver of the turquoise Ford Ranger suddenly awakened from his apparently feigned slumber as I came out of the Ventura County Post building and walked to my Toyota. He started his engine when I started mine and he followed me out of the parking lot and up to Telephone Road where I turned right onto Main Street toward downtown Ventura. He was never more than two car lengths behind me.

Someone needed a few more lessons on the fine art of following.

I took Main Street through midtown to California Street and turned left. There was a place right in front of my office building, a rarity, so I pulled in and killed the Camry's engine. I waited a moment, pretending to get something out of the glovebox, while the guy in the Ranger caught up. He casually ignored me and then parked a few doors down, near the Bombay Bar & Grill.

I climbed out of the car and entered the building. The elevator wasn't there fast enough so I quickly took the stairs to the next floor instead. My office door was the second on the right and I unlocked it and went directly to the window.

The tail was now out of his car, leaning against the passenger side door and looking vaguely my way. He was nearly a block away but I could see that he was Hispanic and a near carbon copy of the five guys who had jumped me in Santa Paula a couple of days ago. He adjusted his red skullcap, pushed back his dark sunglasses and settled back against his truck, trying to look cool and nonchalant. He was neither.

I watched him for a moment. Obviously, he wasn't going anywhere. As long as I wasn't.

I wasn't. I dropped into my chair and put my feet up.

The answering machine was flashing a red "2" so I punched the button to see who had called. The first message was from Bob Kaplan, informing me he'd faxed the *Weapons Grade Charm* contract. A quick glance at the fax machine confirmed it had arrived. The second message was from Johnny Caesar.

"Heller, it's been two days. What's going on? I want an update. Call me. Today."

Caesar was going to have to learn to be patient.

I flipped through my battered Rolodex, picked up the phone and dialed Keith Guillotine, lead singer and spokesman for *Weapons Grade Charm*. As the connection was made, I stood up, stepped over to the window and made sure my tail was still there. He was. Red skullcap and all.

Guillotine answered on the third ring. It was nearly 2:30. Even the musicians were awake.

"Hey, man," Guillotine said. "What's happening?"

"Nothing new and exciting," I told him. "You know, sittin' around the office, answering phones, solving crimes and trying to figure out who's tailing me."

"What?"

"Nevermind, just talking to hear myself talk. Listen, I've got that management agreement. You guys going to be at the rehearsal space today?"

"Yeah, we're supposed to meet there in half an hour."

"Perfect. I'll see you then."

"Awesome! Thanks, Mr. Heller!"

"I told you, call me Brace."

"Thanks, Brace! See you in a little while."

I dropped the phone back into its cradle and wondered briefly if Guillotine was his real name. Probably not.

I went back to the window and peered out. Red Skullcap was polishing the hood of his Ranger but you could tell his heart wasn't really in it. Every few seconds, he'd glance up and make sure the Camry was still there.

I turned away from the window and opened the single grey filing cabinet in the corner, pulled out an empty manila folder, and slipped the *Weapons Grade Charm* contract inside. I tossed it on my desk. Although I hated reading legalese, I knew it was best if I at least briefly went through the *Weapons Grade Charm* contract before I made copies for the band. Kaplan was a great lawyer, but even he sometimes made typos.

A beer sounded good but it was still early so I grabbed a Coke Zero instead, hoping its caffeine would make some sense out of the legal rhetoric. I opened the folder and began reading. *This agreement dated blah blah blah…*

The phone rang. I considered not answering, just in case it was the ever impatient Johnny Caesar, but there are two sounds I can't stand - the caterwauling of a car alarm and a ringing telephone.

"Heller Investigations."

"Heller, Powell." It was Lt. Steven Powell of the Ventura Police Department, a man who never wasted words. "We need to talk."

"When? Where?" I asked. If Powell wasn't going to waste words, neither was I.

"Fifteen minutes. Grant Park."

"Can I bring my tail?"

There was a very brief pause. "You're being fol- lowed?"

"Seems that way."

"Sure. The more the merrier."

"I'll be there."

The line went dead.

CHAPTER ELEVEN

Ten minutes later, I pulled into the cul-de-sac at the top of the mountain where Grant Park was located and parked the Camry next to Powell's beige, government-issue Buick. It was a beautiful day and the view was nothing short of breathtaking. The blue/green ocean stretched out to the hazy horizon like a crystalline carpet and a scattering of whitecaps gave it some definition. The city of Ventura lay splayed out before me, making me think of Prufrock and his patient etherized upon a table. This particular patient, however, was crawling with hundreds of tiny specks that hurried through its streets and sidewalks as the townsfolk went about their daily business.

I stepped out of the Camry and closed the door, taking a deep breath of the cleansing, salt-tinged sea air. A pair of gulls rolled in the sky above me and then dive-bombed a trash barrel, attacking its overflowing fast food wrappers with gusto. Their intensity and determination told me there was some bit of fast food still left in those wrappers as well. The marketing buzzword "cheese paper" zipped through my brain and I quickly pushed it away. The last thing I wanted to think about as I stood and looked out over the beauty of this town was a television commercial for fast food burgers.

Then again, I loved fast food burgers.

I saw Powell's hulking figure sitting at one of the picnic tables overlooking the ocean and started toward him. At the same moment, the turquoise Ford Ranger came rambling up the road, pulling over and parking about a quarter mile away. I pretended not to notice him although it would have taken a blind and deaf man not to. The guy was either really new at this or he really sucked at it.

Powell was finishing a sandwich from the Great Central Steak and Hoagie and my stomach rumbled as I caught the smell of tri-tip and grilled onions. A greasy brown paper bag filled with French fries, one of Great Central's trademarks, lay on the table beside him, fries spilling out in a salty tumble.

I sat down across from him and snatched a couple of fries from the brown paper maw. Powell smiled. "Yeah, help yourself," he said. "It's not like there's not enough of them." His shaved head was tanned a golden brown by the California sun and his dark aviator style sunglasses gave him an evil, James Bond villain appearance. It was an intimidating effect, especially if you were on the wrong side of an interrogation table from him.

I've been there. I know.

"I love that place," I said. "Guess I'll have to have lunch there now."

"Well, it's only ... what? ... two blocks from your office."

"Yeah, walking distance." I sampled another fry. "So what's up?"

Powell shrugged his huge shoulders in the direction of the Ranger. "That your tail?"

I nodded. "You pegged him, huh?"

"Stands out like a sore thumb in a forest of fingers." Powell took a pull on a straw stabbed into a small soda cup emblazoned with the Coca-Cola logo. "You know who it is?"

"Not yet," I said. "Thought I'd see if where he follows me offered any clues."

"And?"

"So far, he's followed me everywhere."

"So much for that theory. Think he's working for Caesar?"

I tried not to seem surprised, and I shouldn't have been. Powell made it his business to know what was going on in his city. And the unusual partnership of Brace Heller and Johnny Caesar was the kind of thing people talked about.

"It's a possibility." I admitted.

"What do you have on that?"

"Nothing, so far." I glanced at my watch. "I've got a meeting in a few minutes and afterwards I thought I'd go out to Rigoberto's and talk to the manager and staff there. See if any of them remember anything from Sunday night."

Powell shook his head. "Better watch your ass. That place is a hotbed for bad guys. And you don't exactly fit the ethnic profile for their usual customer."

"Thought I'd invite Puño along."

"Smart move." Powell ate another fry. "Why'd Caesar come to you?"

"Said he knew I was the best."

"Bullshit. He'd rather have one of his cronies put a bullet in your gut than give you a job. What gives?"

"I honestly don't know."

"And why'd you accept?"

"It's one of those things," I said. "Might need a favor someday."

"A favor a law-abiding citizen couldn't give you."

I gave him a small smile.

Powell took a pull on his soda. "Shit, man. Sometimes I think you got it made, having no one to answer to but yourself. But then you have to go and get in bed with an asshole like Johnny Caesar. Doesn't seem worth it."

"Might not be. He's not exactly known for being a man of his word. We'll have to wait and see." I stole another pair of fries and decided I was going to the Hoagie place next. "Anything you can tell me?"

"About the Garcia boys? Not much you don't already know. I always liked Diego for the murder of that twelve year old in Montalvo, though. Could never pin it on the bastard."

"I remember that. Pissed the hell out of me."

"Yeah. Kid and his mom are just getting home from school and they realize someone's broken in. When the kid goes in the bedroom to call the police, the fucker's still in there. Stabs the kid in the chest and runs out of the house, leaving the mom to deal with her son and his punctured heart. Poor kid bled out in a matter of minutes. No way they could save him."

I felt the hot, dangerous swell of anger returning, warming my stomach. "And you think Diego was the perp."

"I'm pretty sure of it. We have him in the neighborhood that day, he was on one of his drug-induced soirees—we got him on public intoxication nearby a few hours later—and he couldn't really account for his whereabouts in that time period. But we didn't have any witnesses or any evidence ..."

"What about the mother?"

"Do you really think that anyone with their twelve year old son lying on the ground with a knife wound to the heart is going to be good at identifying someone who just ran past them?"

"No. Good point."

"I was sure that fucker did that. And he skated again." He sighed. "Family still calls me every year to find out if we've made any progress."

"Tough call to take," I said.

"You got that right."

Powell ate a French fry and glanced at the Ranger again. "Want me to shake him down?"

"Not yet," I said. "Let's see how far he goes."

Powell scanned the park. "There's like four cars here including yours, mine and your buddy's," he said. "He's obviously going to follow you into the bathroom if you need to go …"

"Well, you know it takes two people to hold it."

"… and apparently, he doesn't care who knows about it." Powell snorted as my line sank in, grinned and shook his head. "Get the fuck out of here."

I stared at him. "Wait a minute. You called me all the way up here just to find out what I knew so far about Diego?"

Powell shrugged his huge shoulders again. "Not really. I called you all the way up here to let you know that I *knew* about you working for Johnny Caesar."

"Thanks."

"Hey, you coulda called and told me," Powell said. "Saved me from calling you." He ran a hand over the bare skin of his head, wiped the sweat off on his jeans.

"Didn't seem necessary."

"Maybe not necessary, but woulda been nice." Powell looked out toward the ocean. I followed his gaze, once again admiring the way the Ventura Pier reached out from the beach into the deep blue sea. "Anyway," he continued, "It's a better view here than from my office."

I had to agree. "Better than mine, too." I reached into

my pocket and pulled out the piece of paper with Ian Kilgore's name and a description of his car on it. I slid it across the table and, since I was there, grabbed another fry. "You ever hear of this guy?"

Powell read the name out loud. "Ian Kilgore? Can't say I have. He in one of those loud ass bands you manage?"

"No. He's been hassling a friend of mine over at O'Leary's. I want to see how dangerous he might be."

"Stalker?"

"Something like that."

Powell took the paper and pushed it into his shirt pocket. "I'll give it a look. Let you know if I find anything."

"Thanks, Steve."

"Tell your tail I said goodbye."

"You got it. Talk to you later."

Powell was eating the last of his fries as I headed back to the Camry. Out of the corner of my eye, I saw Red Skullcap notice my return. As I passed him on the way out of Grant Park, he started the truck and made a U-turn, falling right into place behind me.

CHAPTER TWELVE

The members of Weapons Grade Charm used an abandoned thrift store on Chestnut Street in downtown Ventura as a rehearsal space. It was almost exactly one block from my office so I parked the Camry on California Street (that space right out front was still miraculously open) and walked there.

Red Skullcap had followed me back to the office and, as I started up Main Street toward the rehearsal space, he quickly fell into step about a hundred feet behind me.

As I passed Dargan's Irish Pub & Restaurant on the corner, two doors down and across the street from the rehearsal space, I could already hear the roar of rock'n'roll throbbing from ahead. The band was rehearsing in full force. As I moved nearer, I listened closely, trying to identify the song they were playing. I couldn't put my finger on it, but it all sounded strong. I had a good feeling about this band.

As I approached the empty building and sighted the broken chain hanging from the double glass doors, I wondered if the owners of the place even knew the band was rehearsing there. I opened the door and, instantly, the music intensified. I could feel my pant legs dancing against my shins with the noisy concussion.

A quick glance over my shoulder froze Red Skullcap in his steps. He was standing near the streetlight on Main Street and staring up Chestnut Street at me. When we locked eyes, he suddenly turned and quickly scanned up and down the window at Dargan's, perusing a window menu that I knew wasn't there.

I let the door swing closed behind me and I couldn't even hear the rattle of the heavy chain against the glass due to the deafening roar of the band. They didn't miss a lick, although Keith Guillotine noted my entrance with a nod of his head. They finished the song (a tune I now recognized as "Nights Without You,") with a flourish that would have made any audience jump to their feet and pump their fists in the air.

These guys were the real thing.

"Hey, Brace," Guillotine said, as the song came to an end. "Wanna beer?"

"Sure."

He went to a cooler filled with ice and beer cans and tossed me a Bud Light. It wasn't my favorite, but it would do. I popped the top and took a long drag. It went down smooth and cool.

"Sounding good," I said. Guillotine smiled and waved me to an ancient Formica-topped table with three chairs. His long hair was pulled forward, almost over his face, and it was all slanted to one side, as though it were caught in a constant breeze.

Saint Snider, the guitar player, jerked his head in the direction of the folder as he took one of the three chairs around the table. "That it?" He was shirtless and his head was shaved clean. The baldness was balanced by a full-on hillbilly mustache and a bushy beard that went nearly to his pierced nipples.

"That's it," I said. I opened the folder and pulled out the four copies I had made on the fax machine at the office. I put one in front of each band member and slid the original out in front of me so I could follow as they read along. I set a pen on the table as well.

Guillotine swooped up the pen and quickly scrawled his name on the bottom of the document.

"Don't you want to read it?" I asked him.

"We trust you," he said.

"It's not about trust," I said. "It's about you knowing what this is all about."

"I'll read it later," he said.

Saint Snider took his copy and started reading carefully. The other two, J.D. and J.D.2 (they both had the same initials and used the "2" as a separator) stepped forward and took turns with the pen, signing their names. Neither said anything. Such was my experience with drummers and bass players. They were the quiet ones, with the obvious exception of Gene Simmons of KISS who you can't get to shut the hell up.

Saint Snider put his finger on a word in the contract and, without looking up, asked me, "What's this mean?"

He pointed to a paragraph two-thirds into the document.

I leafed through my copy and quickly read the indicated paragraph. "It means that if a deal comes to you while I'm still your manager then you have to refer the deal to me."

"Why would we want to do that?"

"Because it's the right thing to do. If I'm out there drumming up attention for you guys, there are bound to be less-than-scrupulous people who try to go around me. That wouldn't be fair to me." As Saint Snider considered, I continued. "It's also better for you. It'll protect you from scumbags who will sell you the world but take everything you own. You may get a record deal and you may see some money but you'll wind up owing far more than you can ever pay back. I can protect you from that."

Saint Snider nodded. "Makes sense, I guess," he said. His finger continued down the page.

"What have you got planned for us so far?" Guillotine asked.

"Irons in the fire," I said. "Let's get business out of the way first." Guillotine grinned, nodded and took a pull on his Bud. I followed with my own.

Finally, Saint Snider read to the end of the contract and, apparently satisfied, scribbled his name on the provided line. He passed the document back to me.

"Gentlemen," I said, "It's good to be in business with you." I shook each of their hands firmly. Only Saint Snider's grip seemed unsure.

"What do we do now?" he asked.

"You keep practicing," I told him. "Like there's no tomorrow. We don't want to be caught off guard if we have a showcase or something. Plus, I'll need some CDs and bios on the four of you, and the band. Get those to me as soon as you can."

"That it?"

"For now. I'll take care of everything else. Promotion. Social Media. Newspapers. I'll be in touch soon with the next step."

"Doesn't seem like a whole lot," Saint Snider said.

"Maybe not," I said. "But it is."

Saint Snider nodded reluctantly. I tried to smile encouragingly. It wasn't easy. I don't like being mistrusted. I understand it, but I don't like it.

"Listen, as soon as I have something firm, you guys will be the first to know. Okay? Now get back to work. You want to be on top of your game."

Guillotine shook his head. "We're just about done here," he said. He shot a glance at the others, who nodded their agreement.

"Good enough," I said. "Stay on it, guys. With any luck, I'll be calling you at a moment's notice for a showcase at Bombay or something."

"We'll be ready."

I gave them another encouraging smile and was still somewhat disturbed by the frustrated look on Saint Snider's face. I'd seen it before. It was a form of Buyer's

Remorse. He'd signed the contract and now he was worried that it had been the wrong thing to do. Hopefully, later, I'd make him realize he'd made the right decision.

"All right, guys. I'll see ya." I turned, pushed open the glass doors and stepped back out onto Chestnut Street.

CHAPTER THIRTEEN

As soon as I stepped out of the rehearsal space, I saw Red Skullcap still standing on the corner near Dargan's and staring my way. As I headed toward Main Street, he quickly turned and headed away. I laughed out loud.

I crossed the street and walked down Chestnut toward Main. I had almost reached Dargan's myself when I heard the sound of footsteps coming up fast behind me. My hackles raised and I turned sharply, ready to protect myself.

It was Keith Guillotine. He came to a sudden stop and gave me a careful look.

"Hey, Brace," he said. "Didn't mean to scare you."

I smiled. "No problem. I just didn't know who you were."

"Yeah, sorry. Hey, you wanna get a drink?"

Relieved it was Guillotine and not Red Skullcap running up on me brandishing a butcher knife, I smiled and glanced at my watch. "Actually..." I started.

Guillotine's face fell a little. I sensed that he wanted to talk.

"Yeah, I've got a few minutes," I said. "Where you got in mind?"

Guillotine smiled. "The Sewer?" He meant Sans Souci, a dive bar whose nickname was The Sewer, just down the street. "You know it?"

"Know it? For a while, I practically lived there."

Guillotine laughed. I'm not sure it was funny. We walked through the patio and stepped into the bar.

Shell was tending bar. She shot me with her finger and, without asking, poured me a shot of Makers Mark. "Hey, Brace," she said. "What's your friend drinking?"

"Budweiser," Guillotine told her. He smiled at me as she grabbed a bottle from the cooler and set it on the bar. "I guess you *have* been here before," Guillotine smirked.

"Always start here when there's a show at the Theater." I was talking about the Ventura Concert Theater, just across the street. "You can drink four drinks here for the price of one over there. Makes sense to get started where it's cheaper."

Guillotine laughed. "My girlfriend says you need loan papers to order a drink there."

It was my turn to laugh. "She's not far wrong."

We drank for a moment and watched Shell deal with the other patrons. The best thing about the Sans Souci was the clientele. Sometimes fun, sometimes scary, always interesting.

I took another sip of whiskey and set the now less-than-half-full shot on the bar. "How was practice today?"

"Good, I think," Guillotine said. "We tried out a couple of new songs. They're still pretty rusty. But we've got the popular ones down pretty good."

"That's important," I said. "We don't want to schedule a showcase and then give a shoddy performance. It'll be hard enough getting the important people there in the first place. We fuck it up once and it'll make it all but impossible the next time."

"I hear ya." Guillotine took a pull on his Bud. "So how long you been a cop?"

I laughed a little. "I was never a cop," I said. "Thought about it, but frankly it's a little too regimented for me. I like to make my own schedule." I took another sip of Makers Mark. "Plus, I frigging hate paperwork."

"Cops do a lot of paperwork?"

"Yes. They do."

"But isn't there a lot of paperwork in what you do?"

"Sometimes," I said. "But I can control how much most of the time."

Guillotine nodded, took another sip of his beer. He wrapped both hands around it, either holding it like the microphone he was so used to having in his hands or to keep his palms cool. I thought it would be odd for me to ask and didn't.

"You lived here long?" he asked, pulling that wave of black hair out of his eyes.

"All of my life," I told him. "Born in Santa Paula, grew up in Oxnard and Ventura. Never plan on leaving. Can't even imagine living somewhere else. You?"

"Mostly. I'm originally from L.A. Mom and dad used

to work in the movies. Something to do with props. They were never home. I always felt like we were living in someone else's place. Most of the time, my big sister and I had to fend for ourselves. Then, mom and dad bought a big house in the Oxnard harbor just about the time their work suddenly dried up. Lost the house less than a year after they bought it. They both blamed each other and a little while later, they divorced. I moved out with my sister when I was fifteen."

"How old is your sister?"

"She's six years older than me. I guess that makes her ... twenty-seven now."

"You still live with her?"

"No. I got a little studio out on the Avenue. It's expensive ..."

"What isn't in this town?"

"... but it works for me. Believe it or not, I make enough money delivering pizzas to make the rent."

"Leave you enough for food?"

"Not really, but I got gig money for that. Recycled cans. You can't believe how much recyclable stuff people throw away in this town. I push a cart up and down Main Street and I've got fifty bucks in cans to redeem."

I finished my whiskey and pointed to Guillotine's beer. "Another?" He shook his head. I signaled Shell for the bill.

"Listen," I said. "I can't promise you anything. This business doesn't work that way. But I have a good feeling about *Weapons Grade Charm* and I'm going to do whatever I can to make you guys successful. I can't promise I'll make you the next Guns N'Roses or Metallica—I can't even promise I'll get you a record deal—but I will promise you this: I will do everything in my power to make something happen."

Guillotine's eyes widened and, for a second, I thought they were going to tear up.

"Thanks, Brace."

I tossed a few bills on top of the check that Shell had left and stood up. "It was good talking with you," I told him. "Now get out there and keep practicing."

Guillotine smiled. "I will."

"Good. I'm going to hit the head. I'll catch up with you guys early next week."

"Great. Thanks again, Brace."

"You're welcome."

Guilltoine drained the last few drops of his beer as I stood and stepped away from the bar. We shook hands and he headed toward the front entrance. I turned and walked to the staircase that led to the restrooms. It wasn't that I really needed to go but there was someone up there I wanted to talk to.

My tail. The guy with the red skullcap. He had come in halfway through my conversation with Guillotine and had been watching us in his outstandingly obvious way from the balcony rails above.

I figured it was time we were properly introduced.

74

CHAPTER FOURTEEN

I knew there was only one exit from the balcony and it was down the stairs I was currently climbing. I wondered if the guy in the red skullcap knew. Doubted it.

As I neared the top of the staircase, he came the opposite way, stopping suddenly when he saw me. "'Scuse me," he mumbled, and tried to shoulder past. I grabbed a handful of his shirt and shoved him back against the wall, hard enough so that I heard breath forced out of his lungs. His eyes opened wide in shock and surprise and then narrowed quickly with anger. I saw his right arm twist suddenly and heard a tell-tale *snick*. As the switchblade came in toward my gut, I brought my arm up, our wrists cracked together and the knife went flying over the rail. I heard it thunk into something wooden down below and someone down there cried "What the fuck!"

I thumped the guy on the side of his head hard enough to shake his eyes and then dragged him down the hallway to the bathroom. When he tried to struggle, I thumped him again and the struggles weakened.

There was only space for one in the men's room so I dropped him on the toilet seat, slid in close and slammed the door behind us. I banged the deadbolt into place.

I put my face mere inches from his. The smell of stale cigarette smoke wafted from his mouth. "You've been following me around all day," I growled. Why?"

"I don't know what you're talking about, asshole," he said. A crimson rivulet of blood leaked out of the corner of his mouth as he spoke and he wiped it away with his sleeve.

"The hell you don't. You've been outside my office all day. You followed me to Grant Park ... where I was talking to a *cop* ..." His eyes widened slightly at that. "... and then to the thrift store. So what gives?"

"You've got me confused with someone else, man."

I pinched his ear with my right hand and slammed his head against the wall. Pieces of plaster fell like dusty snow onto his do-rag. The blow was enough to make him totter dizzily on the toilet seat. "I'm not stupid, dickweed, and I'm not in the mood to play games," I said. "Why were you following me?"

"I was ... I wasn't ..."

I re-introduced his head to the wall.

"We can do this all day," I told him. "And it's not going to get any more pleasant from this point on."

"Ritchie the Bean sent me," he said quickly.

Ritchie the Bean? "Why?"

"He just said to watch you. See what you were do-ing."

"Yeah, right. And that's why you tried to stick me out

there in the hall."

"I wasn't going to stick you."

"Bullshit!"

"It was just a reaction, man! You jumped *me*, remember? Ritchie didn't say nothin' about hurting you."

"Why, then?"

"To see what you were digging up on Johnny Caesar's brother."

"Why?"

"I don't know ..."

I reached for his ear again.

"I swear to God I don't know! He said something about you setting him up for it or something. I wasn't paying no attention."

Unfortunately, that made sense. Ritchie the Bean was a paranoid son of a bitch. If someone could make it look like Ritchie was behind Diego's death, the ensuing gang war could only have one outcome: the complete dismantling of Ritchie the Bean's mini-empire and Ritchie's subsequent execution. Ritchie was a small guy in the Ventura County crime scene. Caesar was the major player. That war could only end one way.

"Tell Ritchie if he has any more questions, he should talk to me," I said. "And if I see you following me again, I'll break your legs." I grabbed his shirt and slammed him against the wall one last time. "And if you ever pull a knife on me again," I told him. "I'll give it back to you between the eyes. Got it?"

He nodded. Once, then more vigorously.

He got it.

"Get the fuck out of here," I spat.

I opened the door and stepped out, surprised to see the hallway full of people, with Shell at the front of them all. They all bore varying looks of concern and/or excitement.

"What's going on, Brace?" Shell asked.

"Guy's a little drunk," I said. "I convinced him it was time to call Uber."

Shell gave me a wary look but stepped aside and the patrons behind her split like the Red Sea. The guy in the skullcap threaded between them like a Wall Street criminal doing the walk of shame, then slipped down the stairs and all but ran out of the bar.

Shell gave me another WTF look. I shrugged bashfully.

"You know me," I told her. "I just can't stop myself from helping people."

CHAPTER FIFTEEN

The sunlight was fading away and it was dark in my office. I resisted the temptation to turn on the annoying fluorescent ceiling lights. The tiny desk lamp gave me just enough illumination to see the typically quiet telephone. The cool sea air wafted through the open window, its soothing salt smell cleansing my lungs, and the sounds of traffic were diminishing. It was perfect nap conditions but I had a couple of calls to make first.

First, I called the Ventura Theater and left a voicemail message for Destiny, who did the booking there. I told her I had a new act for her to see and that they would be perfect opening act for Tommy Hogart.

Then, I tried Puño on his cellphone. In the background, I heard what was either the song of a humpback whale or some unlucky person's agonized screams.

Puño wasn't much of a whalewatcher.

"I need some backup," I told him.

"Where?"

"Rigoberto's. Santa Paula."

"You need more than backup, *gringo*," Puño said. "What time?"

"I'm thinking seven."

"I'll be there."

"Thanks."

I pushed down the disconnect button, released it, and dialed Marina's cell.

"Hey, baby," I said in my sexiest voice.

"Who is this?" Marina asked.

"Funny."

Marina laughed her tinkling, tingling laugh. "Hi, honey. What's up?"

"Gonna be a little late tonight. Puño and I are going to Rigoberto's to see if anyone remembers anything about that night."

"Rigoberto's? Why don't you just volunteer for a firing squad?"

"Hence, Puño."

"I know. Be careful."

"I will. How about takeout for dinner?"

"Pick Up Stix?"

"You got it."

We hung up. I noticed that the message light was flashing on my answering machine. I punched the button.

"Gumshoe, it's Powell. Checked out this Kilgore guy. He's only got one hit on his record. Some brawl down at the Red Cove last year. Other than that, he's clean. I know that's probably not much help, but it's all I got. Of course, if you want to go ask him some questions yourself, he lives out on Hurst Street."

He rattled off the address and I quickly typed it into

Notepad, printed it out and popped it into my pocket.

It was six fifteen. Forty-five minutes before I had to meet Puño. A twenty minute drive from the 101 to the 126 to Rigoberto's. That left twenty-five minutes for a nap.

So I napped.

CHAPTER SIXTEEN

Rigoberto's is on the corner of East Harvard and 12th Street and literally shares lot space with La Cabana. A small little dance club, Rigoberto's is better known for booty call than for shaking your booty. It was where the horny went to meet other hornys on lonely Saturday nights.

Because it was a hotbed for passion, it was also a hotbed for crime. Tempers flared easily when one drunken patron thought another drunken patron had stolen his or her date. Ecstasy and pot were as readily available as was the booze behind the bar, which peddled mostly Coronas and cheap tequila shots.

I pulled into the tiny parking lot at about five past seven and parked next to Puño's El Camino. He sat behind the wheel, appearing to be asleep, but anyone who tried to jack him in the parking lot—a favorite pastime here at Rigoberto's—would have discovered otherwise to their violent detriment. I walked over to the driver's side and rapped my knuckles on the partially open window.

Puño opened one eye and looked up at me. "You're late."

"Sorry. Overslept."

Puño shrugged. "At least you have a good reason." He opened the door and stood next to me. "Ready to have some fun?"

"I doubt 'fun' is the right word."

"Maybe not for you," Puño said. "But it works for me."

We walked toward the front entrance.

Like any self-respecting meat market, Rigoberto's was very dark inside. Most of the light came from the neon Corona sign on the back wall of the bar. In the artificial gloom, I could barely see the various beer posters that adorned every wall, most of them featuring matadors and/or buxom babes.

There weren't many customers here yet; it was too early in the evening. Rigoberto's didn't really start hopping until about 11:00 PM, when enough tequila had slipped past enough lips so that everyone looked better than they did at the dinner hour. Or at least they seemed to. Or at least nobody cared.

There were three Hispanic men at the bar, sitting exactly one stool apart from each other so no one would mistake them for gay lovers. They all wore their black hair slicked back on their heads like Antonio Banderas in *Four Rooms*. Each of them had a beer and a tequila shot in front of them, in almost exactly the same positions and consumption levels. I guessed it was tonight's drink special.

Sitting at a booth to the right was a girl in a white dress with frilly laces running around the skirt. She seemed attractive enough from a distance but as we got closer I could see that her heavy make-up created an deceptive optical illusion in the darkness. What appeared to be a princess from the entrance became something more like a wicked witch as we drew nearer. She gave us her best head down, eyes-up, "come hither" look as we approached and we both used our iron will to resist. Never has iron will been so easy to conjure.

There were two more Hispanic women at another booth in the back. One wore an orange blouse with a black skirt decorated with flower designs. The other wore a white spaghetti-strapped top with blue jeans. They were easier to see because of the hanging light that swayed gently over their table. Both were attractive enough not to have to hang out at a place like Rigoberto's but good looks didn't always mean good sense and lonely is lonely.

Puño and I finally reached the bar, pulled out stools and sat. Unlike the others, we didn't leave an empty stool between us. They probably figured that we were the gay lovers they were so desperately trying not to be.

The bartender was a doughy Mexican with a faded Kenny Rogers t-shirt that looked out of place here. He thought we looked out of place here, too, and made sure we were aware of it by first giving me an ugly, blistering scowl and then offering Puño a less potent version of it. "Getcha?" he asked.

"What kind of tequila you got?" I said.

"Montezuma," he said. "Maybe some Cuervo. I'll have to go look."

"Forget it. What about beer? Anything on draught?"

"No."

"Bottles then."

"Corona. Dos Equis. Heinekin."

"Heinekin? Really?" I looked at Puño. He widened his eyes in surprise.

The bartender shrugged. "Getcha?" he asked again.

"I'll take a Corona." I told him.

"Same for me," said Puño.

The bartender turned slightly away from us and opened the door to a stainless steel cooler behind the bar. Cool air seeped out from within. I saw Puño's neck lift up as he glanced down into the cooler, making sure that only beer was coming back out.

A pair of Coronas thumped on the counter before us. Using a bottle opener I couldn't see buried in his fleshy hands, the bartender quickly flicked off the lids. "Seven bucks," he said. I threw a ten on the counter and sipped the beer. Not bad.

"*¿Está el encargado adentro esta noche?*" Puño asked suddenly.

"*Soy el encargado,*" said the bartender.

"*¿Cómo te llamas?*"

"*¿Por qué deseas saber?*"

Puño's eyes narrowed slightly. The temperature in the

room seemed to drop by five full degrees. Even the jukebox chose that moment to switch to another song and the silence, except for the mechanical clacking of the machine loading another CD, was devastating.

It was especially impressive because I didn't have a clue as to what they were saying.

"*¿Cómo te llamas?*" Puño asked again, more slowly than before. And this time with feeling. I didn't understand much Spanish but I knew Puño was asking the same question again and was already getting tired of repeating himself.

The bartender saw his future in Puño's eyes and didn't like it. "*Me llamo Carlos*," he said. "*Por que?*"

"Man here is a detective," Puño said, switching to English for my benefit. "Wants to ask you a few questions. Be in your best interest to answer them."

"This about Diego Garcia?" Carlos said.

"Why you ask?"

"Cops been buggin' my ass all week. I'm sick of answering questions."

"Well, you ain't done yet," Puño informed him.

Carlos tried to shrug fearlessly but couldn't quite pull it off. He gladly turned his attention away from Puño and on to me. He didn't seem as frightened of me. It would come. He just didn't know me yet. "What?" he asked bluntly.

"You work Saturday night?"

"Course. Busiest night of the week. You think I get

that off?"

"I don't know. You could have been sick or something."

"No. I was here."

"What went down?"

"Nothing went down. Homeboy comes in, like he does every Saturday, starts demanding free drinks, even though he knows Angel ain't gonna charge him for shit. Never does."

"Angel?"

Carlos rolled his eyes. "The owner?" he said, as if I should have known that going in. He didn't add "duh" but I think he wanted to.

"Angel and Diego friends?"

"Fuck no. Angel only met him once and that's when Diego set up the protection for him way back when."

"What's he charge him?"

"Two grand a month."

"Pretty expensive."

"Cheaper than not having it," Carlos said. "Cheaper than having the place burn down."

"So you didn't notice anything different Saturday night? It was business as usual?"

"Just as always," Carlos said. "Diego comes in here, starts throwing his weight around, hitting on women, drinking free beer, free tequila. End of the night, he's over in his corner ..." He pointed to the booth where the girls were sitting now. "... shit-faced as always. He gets up, spits on the floor and he's fuckin' out of here."

"See anybody new here that night? Anybody who shouldn't have been here?"

"Shit, man. It was *Saturday night*. I was too fuckin' busy to be looking at people's faces."

"There was that one white guy," one of the three amigos at the bar said suddenly.

"Fuck him," Carlos spat. "He don't mean nothing."

"A white guy?" I asked.

"It's nothing, man," Carlos said. "He was looking for La Cabana. The *güeros* love that fuckin' place."

"Yes," I said. "We do."

Carlos' eyes flicked over to Puño. "Didn't mean no disrespect."

"Don't worry about it," I said. "I'm sure you don't get a lot of *güeros* in here. So what'd this guy do?"

"The white guy? He came in, asked me if I knew where La Cabana was. I told him, 'Shit, man, this is Rigoberto's. La Cabana says 'La Cabana' on it. Don't you speak English?'"

The irony wasn't lost on me.

Carlos continued. "He turned round and got the hell out of here before he got his ass beat."

I heard the opening peals of Deep Purple's "Smoke on the Water" and realized my cellphone was ringing. I snapped it off my belt and glanced at the screen.

Even though it had been at least three years since I last spoke with him, I recognized the number. It was

Ritchie the Bean calling. Interesting. I hit the cancel button and let the voicemail pick up the call.

"So when'd you last see Diego that night?"

"I told you already, man. After he got all liquored up and headed for home."

"What time was this?"

"Two-ish. Closing time."

I reached into the pocket of my t-shirt and pulled out a card. I put it on the bar and slid it over to Carlos. He glanced at it but wouldn't touch it. Puño gave him a look and he decided he'd better pick it up after all.

"Do me a favor," I said. "You remember anything unusual, about anything—this white guy, the clothes Diego was wearing, anyone who was talking with him— you give me a call. I would appreciate it."

"I'm not going to remember anything else," Carlos said, looking Puño's way nervously.

My phone gave a little chime. Ritchie had left a message.

"But if you do," I told Carlos. "I would greatly appreciate it."

"Yeah. Whatever. Okay."

I left the change from my ten on the bar and Puño and I walked out. Everyone watched us leave with casual, almost disconnected, disinterest.

As the door closed behind us, I'm pretty sure the party continued in earnest.

CHAPTER SEVENTEEN

There were two suspicious looking teenagers peeking in the half-open window of Puño's El Camino when we got back to the parking lot. Puño was right behind them when he barked out, "Help you?" in a deep, authoritative voice. The two teens looked up suddenly, blanched, and beat a fast path out of the lot.

Laughing, Puño pulled open the door and dropped in.

"They take anything?" I asked.

"Nothing to take," Puño said. "Got the radio on eBay for ten bucks. They want that, they can have it."

I leaned against the truck bed. "This may have been a waste of time."

"Without talking to everyone that was there that night," Puño said, "You're stuck with a lot of open questions. And maybe no answers."

I shrugged. "Well, we had to ask."

"Yes, we did."

I held up my cellphone. "Ritchie the Bean called while we were in there."

"The hell does he want?"

"I forgot to tell you about the little gift he sent me today." I filled him in on my new friend in the red skullcap.

Puño laughed. "That's funny. Ritchie's so stupid he didn't think you'd make the guy."

"Stevie Wonder would have made this guy," I said. I opened the phone and pushed the button for voicemail, then hit the speakerphone function. After the droning robot told me I had once voicemail message, I heard Ritchie's voice come through.

"Hey, Heller, Ritchie here. Look, I know it's been a long time since we talked and, uh, I'm sorry about that bozo I sent to look after you today. Guy wouldn't know how to tail a dog." He snorted a little laugh that sounded tinny and false over the tiny phone speaker. "Anyways, give me a call sometime and let's talk about this Diego Garcia thing. I wanna offer you any help I can. And, like I said, man, I'm sorry about the guy following you today."

The droning robot told me I had no more voicemail messages.

I glanced at my watch. It was 7:35. "You got anything going tonight?" I asked Puño.

"*Nada.*"

"Wanna go see Ritchie the Bean with me?"

Puño rolled his eyes. "I forgot," he said. "I'm supposed to go home and wash my hair."

CHAPTER EIGHTEEN

Ritchie the Bean lived in a glorious home built in the early 1900s that clung to the hillside of Santa Paula where Ritchie could overlook the city and tell his never-ending parade of visitors—which included Peruvian drug lords and local heads of state—how much of the city below he controlled.

Had he been more of an honest man, Ritchie would have confessed that he controlled very little. Most of his money (and he had plenty of it), came from his family who had hit it big in the motion picture industry back in the '60s making low budget films loaded with motorcycles, drug use and frequently topless women. The small percentage of Santa Paula's criminal world owned by Ritchie was more of a hobby than anything else. It gave him a sense of power that his failed attempts at carrying on the family business—making a string of bad horror movies in the 80s—did not.

A pair of bored security guards leaned sleepily on each of the brick pillars that book-ended the gate to Ritchie's home. Both guards wore blue jeans and matching t-shirts with "Silver Security" printed in bold white letters across the back.

Both had a handgun unceremoniously stuffed into the front of their pants. Not my favorite way to carry a gun; I don't like the direction the barrel is pointing.

As rich as he was, Ritchie was too cheap to build a guard kiosk so the guards merely stood by the gate, awaiting potential visitors. As we approached in Puño's El Camino, the guards stirred and their hands moved nearer to the butts of their guns.

Puño brought the El Camino to a halt and smiled brightly at the guard on his side. "We're here to see Ritchie."

The guard leaned down and stared first at Puño and then shifted his eyes to me. The guard on my side didn't budge.

"Who's *we*?" said the first guard.

"Girl Scouts," Puño said happily. "We got his cookie order."

The guard didn't think that was funny.

"Brace Heller," I said, passing a card across Puño to the guard. He took it and eyed it suspiciously. "This is Puño. Ritchie knows us. He's expecting us."

The guard glared at us for another moment, then turned his back to us as he pulled a walkie-talkie off of his belt. As he turned, the other guard became suddenly more alert.

I still figured that Puño and I could take them.

We didn't have to. The first guard lowered his walkie-talkie and signaled to the other. The second guard touched a remote control attached to his belt and the big wrought iron gate in front of us squeaked open.

"Put you down for a box of Pecan Sandies?" Puño asked the guard as we drove in. He got a single finger as a response.

"Did he mean just one box?" Puño asked me as we headed up the main drive.

"Yeah," I said. "That's what he meant."

Ritchie the Bean met us on the front porch of his small mansion, watching us with a serious, business-like stare as we climbed out of Puño's car and came toward him. Ritchie was almost seventy years old but the few strands of hair left on top of his head were still jet black ... and he didn't dye it. He needed glasses to see but vanity kept him from wearing them. The result was a permanent squint. Ritchie wasn't a big man but he was just overweight enough to seem puffy and doughy. He wore a white jogging outfit with white socks and white tennis shoes. It was that look that had given him his nickname, although it didn't really make any sense. Ritchie had originally been called "Ritchie the Vanilla Bean," because he always wore white. It had been shortened to "Ritchie the Bean" in recent years. I never understood any of it because all the vanilla beans I've ever seen are actually brown like beef jerky.

Ritchie held out a liver-spotted hand as we reached the final steps to the porch and we shook. His grip was firm but his skin was the smooth skin of a man who counted money but never did any real work. "Brace. Mr. Puño. It's good to see you both. Have a seat."

For some reason, Ritchie always called me "Brace" and Puño "Mr. Puño." Something else about Ritchie that I never understood.

We walked up the steps to the porch and Ritchie indicated a trio of white Rattan chairs with vinyl cushions and the three of us sat. I felt more like I was at an estate in the richer part of New Orleans than in the hills of Santa Paula.

"Lemonade? Something stronger?" Ritchie asked. "Maria makes a *killer* Mint Julep." I could see from the water rings on the glass table between us that Ritchie had been enjoying a few already.

"I'm good," I said, the Nawlins feeling growing.

"Got any *cerveza?*" Puño asked.

Ritchie turned to a young Mexican woman standing behind him. "Maria, a *Modelo* for my friend, please." The way Ritchie watched her as she walked away told me she was more than a retriever of refreshments.

Finally, Ritchie tore his eyes away from Maria's bottom and turned gravely to me. "Listen, Brace, I'm sorry about that tail. Fuckin' guy. Couldn't follow his dick if it wasn't in front of him."

"Yeah, what was that about?" I asked him. "You want to know something, Ritchie, you should give me a call."

"I know, I know. I said sorry, didn't I? It's just that I

95

heard you were looking into who shot Diego Garcia ..."

"I am."

"...and I couldn't afford somebody tying me into it."

"Why? You got something to do with it?"

"Christ, no!" Ritchie spat vehemently. Maria had arrived with the drinks and she almost spilled them when she flinched a little at Ritchie's indignant response. She recovered quickly, however, and passed a Negro Modelo to Puño and placed a Mint Julep on the table beside Ritchie. "I knock off Johnny Caesar's brother and it's war. I don't want war with Johnny Caesar."

"Be a short ass war," Puño smirked.

"Maybe, maybe not." Ritchie gave Puño what he thought was a withering glare. Puño's complete indifference told him it wasn't so withering.

With a wave of his hand and a nod of unfelt thanks, Ritchie dismissed Maria. "Point is, I don't want a war with Johnny Caesar." He sipped at his new Mint Julep. "What the hell you doing working for Johnny anyway?" he asked.

"He hired me."

"Why don't you ever do any work for me?"

"You never asked," I said. "What do you know about who killed Diego?"

Ritchie took another sip of his Mint Julep and made a face like he was having an orgasm. It was something I could never unsee. "Goddamn, that's good." He held it over the table. "Here, try this. I'm telling you, it's the best goddamn Mint Julep you ever had."

I declined but Puño tried a sip and nodded in agreement. "Pretty damn good," he said.

"Ritchie, what do you know about who killed Diego?" I repeated.

"I don't know anything," he said, displeased that I would even ask when he was drinking the Mint Julep to end all Mint Juleps. He took a big gulp, draining half of it. "Why would I?" He snapped his fingers loudly. "Maria! Bring me another one!"

"You got people on the ground," I said. "They see anything?"

"I told you, I don't know anything. All I know is what I read in the papers. Somebody clipped Johnny Caesar's brother. It wasn't me. I'm sorry for the poor bastard who did it. Johnny won't rest until the guy's farting dust."

"You don't have any ideas? Any theories? Any suspicions?"

Ritchie shook his head. "I got nothing, Brace, swear to God." He finished the Mint Julep in his hands just as Maria arrived with another. Ritchie took it hungrily. "I suppose he told you about the contract."

"What contract?"

Ritchie's eyebrows climbed in surprise. "Been a contract out on Johnny's head for about three months now. He told you that, right?"

"This is the first I've heard of it," I said.

"Well, you didn't hear it from me."

"How do you know about this?"

Ritchie gave me a pained look. "I gotta know. It's how I stay alive."

"All right. So who put out the contract?"

"Don't know."

"Don't know or won't tell?"

"Don't know, Brace. Christ, you know I'll talk to you. I just don't know. Last time I talked to Johnny, he said he didn't know either." His new Mint Julep was disappearing fast.

"You think Diego's murder is tied into this contract?"

Ritchie shrugged. "Could be," he said. "Maybe the shooter made a mistake. Johnny and Diego are brothers. They kinda look alike."

"Yeah, like Bill and Roger Clinton," Puño grunted.

"But there is a resemblance," I said. "You think the shooter got the wrong guy?"

"Stranger things have happened." Ritchie held his now nearly empty glass against his lower lip, enjoying the cool rim. The ice shifted and tinkled playfully against the glass. Ritchie's eyes began to blur with alcoholic disinterest. "Funny he didn't tell you about the contract," he said.

"Yeah," I agreed. "Hilarious." I stood. Puño downed his beer and followed suit. "Thanks, Ritchie. You hear about anything, give me a call, all right?"

"Listen, Brace," Ritchie said. His words were beginning to slur. He was either a lightweight or he'd been drinking long before we arrived. "I want you to promise me you'll keep me out of this."

"If you don't have anything to do with it, Ritchie, then I'll keep you out of it."

"I don't," Ritchie said, blinking rapidly. "I swear to God, I don't."

"Then you've got nothing to worry about."

"Thanks, Brace. Thanks, man." He drained the last of his Mint Julep and collapsed into his chair, giving us a half-assed wave of goodbye. "Maria! Where's that Mint Julep, goddammit!"

On the way back to La Cabana to get my car, Puño said, "You got a real big mess on your hands if some outside shooter came in to take out Johnny Caesar and capped his brother instead."

I nodded. "A lot depends on who hired that outside shooter. This could turn big and ugly real fast."

"*Real* fast," Puño agreed. "I wonder if that white guy at Rigoberto's that night is our guy?"

"Don't know," I replied. "But I doubt that Rigoberto's has security cameras so we can go back and take a look."

"Yeah," Puño said. "I doubt it."

Pick Up Stix was closed by the time I got there so I drove over to In-N-Out and bought three burgers and two fries. When I got home, Marina was laying on the couch, reading a celebrity magazine and streaming *Game of Thrones* on HBO Go.

"How many times are you gonna watch that??" I asked her.

"As many as I want," she shot back. She eyed the In-N-Out bag. "No Pick Up Stix?"

"Sorry," I said. "We ran a little late. It was closed when I got there."

Marina shrugged. "In-N-Out's always good." She plucked a fry from the box and ate it nimbly. "But I had my heart set on Pick Up Stix."

"I know," I told her. "Tomorrow."

We spread out our feast and dug in. She was right. In-N-Out is always good. But I'll take the Steak & Hoagie's fries over In-N-Out's any day.

"So how'd it go at Rigoberto's?" Marina asked around a mouthful of French fries.

"Not so good," I told her. "Apparently, the Latino hotties there don't like their white guys big and ugly. I couldn't even get one dance."

She threw a fry at me and it bounced off. Wurzel pounced on it and ate it furiously.

"We didn't learn anything," I told her. "Bartender claims he didn't see anything unusual. They all say that. Then we took a drive up to see Ritchie the Bean ..."

Marina gave me a curious look.

"He called, so we paid him a visit. He wanted us to keep him out of this."

100

"Will you?"

"If he didn't do it. If he did, he's on his own."

I scraped some cheese off my burger wrapper with a French fry and ate it. Angels sang in the heavens.

"We also found out that someone's got a contract out on Johnny Caesar. Wonder if the shooter got the wrong guy."

"Why didn't Johnny tell you that?"

"I'll ask him tomorrow. Maybe he just didn't think there was a connection."

We finished our burgers and fries and watched the rest of *Game of Thrones*. As usual, I had no idea what was going on but Marina was enthralled. Again. After it was over, I grabbed the remote and turned off the TV.

"Now what?" Marina asked.

"Well," I told her. "All that medieval sex and violence has me all hopped up."

"Most of it was gay," Marina said.

"Yes," I said. "But not all of it."

CHAPTER NINETEEN

I was deep in a post-coital sleep when the phone shrill shocked me out of it like a drowning infant yanked out of the family pool. As I scrambled for the phone, I realized that Marina was gone—her side of the bed was neatly made, as usual—and Wurzel had curled into a warm ball just beneath her pillow.

"Yeah," I growled into the phone.

"Brace!" Kristyn's voice stabbed into my ear. "Brace, he's ...!"

There was a crash and the line went dead.

I leapt out of bed, grabbed the Sig Sauer and ran for the door.

Five minutes later, I slid the Camaro into O'Leary's empty parking lot and slammed on the brakes. I jumped out of the car, not bothering to close the door, and ran to the bar. In my peripheral vision, I saw that Kristyn's VW was the only car in the parking lot.

The door was locked, but the glass in it was cracked in a spider web pattern. I used the butt of the Sig Sauer to knock a fist-sized hole in the glass and reached in and unlocked the door from the other side.

KNIFEPOINT

As soon as I stepped in, I noticed the knife on the floor beside the door. It was a hunting knife, a mean looking one. I knelt down and looked at it closely. There didn't appear to be any blood.

I stood and listened carefully. The place seemed empty. Then I heard the soft sounds of a woman whimpering coming from behind the bar. I jumped over the counter and found Kristyn lying there, in a fetal position, mewing like a frightened kitten.

"Kristyn, it's Brace," I said. "Is he still here?" I scanned her quickly for any cuts or bruises, didn't see any.

Kristyn sprang off the floor and grabbed me in a clutching bear hug. And then the sobbing began.

"It's okay, honey," I told her. "Is he still in here?"

She shook her head, gasped to get her breath. "No," she said. "He didn't get in."

"What happened?"

She took a deep, shuddering breath and I helped her to her feet. "I went out to my car after we closed," she said. "And he was hiding in the back seat. He grabbed me by the hair and he had a knife." She stopped and took a deep hitching breath. "He told me ..." she started. The words caught in her throat.

"Go ahead, sweetheart ..."

"He told me he was going to ... going to f..."

"It's okay, Kristyn, I'm here."

"He said he was going to fuck me and then kill me, Brace." Her voice caught again. "That's the word he used.

And he said other, filthier things. Then he started to climb over the seat and I ran. I *ran*. I keep my work keys on my belt and I was able to get to the door and get it open but he was right behind me. I closed the door on his arm and he dropped the knife and I was able to get it closed and locked. Then he broke the glass ..."

"But he didn't get in."

"Somebody drove past and he ran off." She took another breath and looked into my eyes. "I don't think he would have stopped otherwise, Brace."

"He'll stop now," I told her.

We called Kristyn's boss and waited for him to show up before I helped Kristyn get back into her car and then followed her to her mother's house on the other side of town. She drove slowly and swerved a little every now and then. I knew she was probably still in some sort of shock.

I would have walked her to the door when we got to her mother's house but, at some point on the drive over, I realized I was still wearing just my boxer shorts. Kristyn came over to the window, leaned in and gave me a quick kiss on the cheek.

"I'll be all right, Brace," she told me. "Thank you."

"Get some sleep," I said. "And try not to think about this."

"I'll try."

"And take a few days off. Go to Santa Barbara or

Catalina or something. Stay away from work. Call me in a few days and we'll talk."

She gave my bicep a quick squeeze. "Thanks, Brace."

She walked to the front door, opened it with the key and gave me a shy little wave as she closed the door behind her.

I drove back home and put on some pants. Then I headed over to Ian Kilgore's place.

I eased the Camaro casually past Kilgore's duplex on Hurst Street. Kilgore's monster Caddy sat in the driveway and I assumed that meant Kilgore had made it home. I also assumed he was sitting by the window, possibly with a gun, waiting for the police to arrive.

Or maybe he'd try to play it cool and casual. "What do you mean, officer? She wanted it. She was hot for me." The son of a bitch.

The night was almost completely silent as I parked the Camaro one street over on South Pacific and crept through the back yard of the house directly behind Kilgore's. I figured he'd be peering out the front window, waiting for the police, and I hoped he wouldn't think about the back. The early morning silence and moonless night were my enemies. Every sound I made—opening a gate, climbing a short fence, my shoes crunching on gravel—seemed amplified a thousand times and, even though my eyes had adjusted to the darkness, everything was in shades of blue, black and grey. It was difficult to see exactly where I was going.

Thankfully, except for a lonely dog a few streets over, Ventura slept.

Finally, I dropped over the brick wall dividing the two buildings and found myself in Kilgore's back yard. A short wooden fence separated his yard from the other side of the duplex and I stayed low behind it in case his neighbor decided to come out for a moonlight cigarette.

I stepped up three concrete steps to the back door and gently clicked open the screen door. I put my hand on the door knob and gently turned.

Locked, of course.

I had two options now. One: I could use the pick in my pocket to jimmy the lock (and I could do it but it might be a little noisy and would take time I didn't have). Two: I could just knock the goddamn door off its hinges (and that would bring the cops a lot more quickly and would seriously limit my quality time with Mr. Kilgore).

I decided that the important thing about my time with Mr. Kilgore was the *quality* rather than the *quantity* and I stepped back and rammed my shoulder into the door. These were older places here on Hurst Street and the door gave way easily with minimal noise.

Of course, even a deaf person would have heard the crash at 3:30 in the morning.

I rushed through the tiny kitchen of the small duplex into the bedroom/living room, scanning every corner as I made my way and discovered that Kilgore wasn't at the front window where I thought he'd be. Instead, he was in bed, probably pretending to be asleep.

He wasn't pretending any more. As I rushed into the room, he sat up suddenly and struck out with what, in the dim blue blackness of the room, looked like another of those nasty hunting knives.

It was easy to knock the knife away (it clattered noisily and harmlessly to the floor), and I grabbed a handful of Kilgore's hair. I yanked him out of the bed and pushed him up against the wall, making sure his head banged painfully against it. Then I screwed the barrel of the Sig Sauer up high into his right nostril.

"Wh ... What?" Kilgore managed. His breath stank of stale alcohol and cigarettes.

"Don't you dare insult me by pretending you don't know what this is about," I snarled. I could feel the anger inside me like a caged beast, beating at the bars of my rib cage and begging for release. "I'll blow your head all over this room and not think twice about the mess, you understand?"

He nodded as best he could with my forearm pressed against his throat. I liked the way his face looked as he struggled to take another breath so I put some more pressure behind it.

"You will stay away from Kristyn and you will stay away from O'Leary's and we will never see each other again, you got it?"

Nod.

"Because if you don't, because if I see you anywhere near her or that bar, I will find you and I will kill you and I will cut your body into pieces and feed it to the sharks out by the Channel Islands. Do we understand one another?"

Another nod. This one weaker.

"Ian, I want you to know this is serious. I'm not one for kidding or playing games. If you don't do as I say, exactly as I say, I will do what I promise. Do you understand that?"

He nodded. Definitively, this time.

"Let's hope we don't run into each other again."

I pushed him onto the floor and, as he gasped for breath behind me, I walked out the front door into the night.

I jogged down Hurst Street and around the corner to South Pacific. Lights were on in some of the houses now but nobody seemed to pay any attention to me as I ran by. As I climbed into the Camaro, a red tumble of police lights stained the night sky, telling me that the cops had arrived at Ian's right behind me.

I started the engine and I wondered what he would tell them about his late night visitor.

CHAPTER TWENTY

It had been a night short on sleep so when I put the key in my office door the next morning, it took me longer than it should have to realize it had been jimmied. I was too tired to reach for my gun and was in dire need of the Diet Coke in my other hand so I just leaned on the door and hoped that whoever had broken in wasn't planning on shooting me.

The waiting area was empty but through the opaque glass that separated the two rooms I could see three blurry figures—two standing, one sitting—inside my office space. I put the Diet Coke on the reception desk, wearily drew the Sig Sauer and walked through the door.

Johnny Caesar sat at my office desk with his two bodygoons standing at attention beside him like tumescent bookends. Johnny stared back at me with a manufactured look of boredom. He wasn't fooling anybody.

I slid the Sig Sauer back into its holster and walked right past the bodygoon on the right. He tensed up but didn't make a move toward me.

"It's been three days, Heller," Caesar said. "What you got?"

"You guys got it all wrong," I said. "See, *I'm* the detective and I sit here." I pointed at my desk chair. "You're the *client* and the client sits here. This is why they call it the *client chair*." I held my hands like Carol Merrill and indicated the chair on the opposite side of the desk. "And, you, two ..." I said to Johnny's bodyguards, "...well, you're meaningless, so you should wait outside."

The guards bristled. It was kinda cute.

"Cut the shit, Heller," Caesar spat. "What's going on?"

"Get the hell out of my chair and we'll talk."

"I'm fine where I am."

"Yeah, well I'm not. This is my office and that's my chair. Clients sit on the other side. You want an update, you move your ass over there."

Caesar glared at me a moment and then shrugged. He got up slowly and moved to the client's chair. The bodygoons followed him, taking up their positions automatically, staring at me with looks that did not send good wishes. I took my place at the desk, rocked back, rested my legs on the desktop.

"So?" Caesar urged.

"So, I got nothing."

If Caesar had been drinking, he would have spit-sprayed it all over me. "Nothing? You got nothing?! Three days after I paid you, and you still don't have shit?"

"Johnny, this is a *murder* investigation," I said. "You didn't really expect me to solve the goddamn thing in three days, did you?"

"Maybe not solve it, but I expected you to have *something*. What'd you get from those punks in Santa Paula?"

"What punks?"

"The ones you roughed up in the field. The field they found Diego in."

"You having me watched, too, Johnny?"

"Whattaya mean, 'too'? Who else is having you watched?"

"You got somebody following me? That wasn't our agreement."

"Hey, man, I'm paying you a lot of money. I'm just making sure you're out there doing your job."

"First of all, you've only paid me a retainer and I've already incurred expenses beyond that. Secondly, if you don't think I'm doing my job, then fire me."

"Who else is tailing you?" Caesar spat angrily.

"Better yet, I quit. I don't need this shit," I said. "Get somebody else. I'm out. You owe me about a hundred bucks over and above the retainer so far but let's just call it even and go our separate ways."

"Hey, fuck that ..."

"And why didn't you tell me about this contract that's out on you, Johnny? That's what I call need-to-know information. I had to find that out on my own, wasting my time and *your* money doing it. Maybe that's why I'm taking so long in finding out anything. I'm too busy covering ground you should have covered from the beginning."

I could see the two bodygoons increase minutely in size as they both took deep breaths, anticipating their boss instructing them to rip me apart. But Johnny surprised them. "Go wait outside," he told them.

It took a moment for his instruction to sink into their fat heads. "Outside!" Caesar barked and they finally, reluctantly, did as they were told.

As the door closed behind them, Caesar turned back to me. "You shouldn't talk down to someone in front of their employees."

"You shouldn't have come in here with a chip on your shoulder," I said. "And without a key."

"I'll pay for the fuckin' lock, okay?" Johnny said. "You gotta understand, Heller, my little brother's dead. I'm more than a little upset by this whole thing. I want to know who done this."

"And I'll find out, if I can," I told him. "But I need you to do what you said you'd do. I'll repeat myself: I don't want anybody following me. Anybody. Your guys, somebody else's guys, not even Halle Berry. I can't work that way. If it happens again, I'm done."

"Who else was tailing you?"

"I'm not going to tell you that. It doesn't concern you. What concerns you is keeping your end of the bargain."

"All right. I'm sorry. I told ya, I'm fuckin' upset,

okay?"

"Okay," I said. "Now tell me more about this contract."

Caesar sat back, and sighed deeply. "I first heard about it about three weeks ago. One of my guys on the street heard it from somebody else. Obviously, when you hear a rumor that someone's out to cap you, you take it seriously."

"Obviously."

"Anyway, I checked around and my guy wasn't the only guy who heard it." He smiled grimly. "So far, it ain't happened, you know what I mean?"

"That's all you know? You don't know who put it out? How real it is?"

"That's all I know."

"Why didn't you tell me?"

"Didn't seem important."

"Your little brother gets gun downed on your own turf when there's a contract out on you and you don't think it's important?"

Caesar's look hardened. "You think someone got him instead of me?"

"I think it's possible."

"I didn't even think of that."

"That's why you should have told me. Now, is there anything else I need to know?"

Caesar's mind was working. I could see his eyes take their focus off of me as the wheels turned. There was something there and I was eager to see if he'd share it but I wasn't surprised when he said, "Nah, that's it. I got nothing else, Heller."

"Then get the hell out of here and let me get to work," I said. "And don't call me. I'll call you. When I have something."

"You do that," Caesar said. He sat for a moment, still thinking, and then suddenly rose and walked to the door.

"And don't forget to fix the lock."

"Yeah, yeah, I'll send a guy," Caesar said, and stepped into the hallway. The two bodygoons fell in step behind him.

I got up and went into the front office where I retrieved my Diet Coke. It had left a ring of condensation on the desk there and I wiped it away with the palm of my hand. As I headed back to my desk, I noticed the flashing light on the answering machine and hit the play button.

"Brace, it's Destiny over at the Ventura Theater. We haven't set an opener for Tommy Hogart yet so send me a package on your guys. If they're okay, maybe we'll give 'em a shot. Hope all's well, man."

Well, that was good news. I decided I'd better call Keith Guillotine and find out where the hell those promo packages were.

CHAPTER TWENTY-ONE

Once again, I found my mind wandering to the late Erle Stanley Gardner and the fictitious Perry Mason. There I sat, in the same building that the former had actually worked out of and that the latter was arguably created in, and, like those two, I was awash in a sea of crime and mystery.

Unlike the author and his creation, however, I had only questions and no answers.

Who had killed Diego Garcia? Was it a targeted assassination or a case of mistaken identity? Did my lack of any solid leads or sound theories speak to the difficulty of solving the case or did I just not care enough? Where did I go next? How was I going to move forward?

What was I going to have for lunch?

I looked at the clock on my desk. It was 10:15. The morning sun was just starting to warm the night's chill out of the office. That meant it was a long time until lunch. Just as well. I had no ideas on that subject, either.

The front door creaked open and someone stuck their head inside. Through the opaque glass between my office and the reception area, I could see only that it was a woman. Her long black hair spilled over her shoulder as she shyly peeked into the reception area and then took a moment before inching in.

A client? At this time of the morning? At last, someone to while away the hours with until lunchtime! Maybe a pizza from Tony's Pizzaria. Or a chili cheese dog from Wienerschnitzel.

Or a salad at Meridian's Cafe, said the voice of Marina in my head.

Pushing away thoughts of lunch, I stood, straightened my shirt and belt as best I could, walked over and opened the door.

The woman in the reception area gave a little flinch as I stepped through the door and offered her a welcoming smile. Then she quietly closed the outer door behind her and said, with an accent that made it clear English was her second language: "You are Mr. Heller?"

"I am," I told her. "Please, come inside."

She stared at me warily for a moment and then slipped past me into my office. Her brown skin was clear and smooth and her Hispanic heritage apparent. She wore a pair of black slacks, a lacy button up blouse and open toed shoes. None of it looked expensive, but it didn't look cheap, either. I was thinking Old Navy rather than Walmart. She walked over to my desk and stood by the client chair, waiting for me to tell her what to do next.

"Please," I said, closing the door behind me, "Have a seat."

She hesitated a moment as though she was uncertain

whether she should really even be there, and then sat down in the client chair. "Get you a cup of coffee?" I asked her. "A Coke, maybe?"

"No," she said quietly. "Thank you."

I decided not to ask her if she wanted a shot of the Makers Mark in my bottom drawer. At least not yet. Instead, I walked around and sat behind my desk, resisting the urge to sit back and put my feet up on the desk. I was a professional, after all.

"What can I do for you, Miss ...?"

"Alvarez," said the woman, "Elva Alvarez."

"Miss Alvarez ..."

She hesitated again, gathering her thoughts and, I believe, her courage. "They say you are looking for who killed Diego Garcia."

"Who's 'they'?"

This brought a moment of confusion to her. She thought carefully, mentally translated her response into English and said, "People. No one in particular. I just ... heard that."

I nodded, impressed with her careful pronunciation of 'particular.' "That would be correct," I said. "I have been hired by his brother to find out who killed him."

Elva stared at me silently. I couldn't tell whether the wheels of her mind were working again or if she was struggling with the news that I had been hired by Caesar.

"You just missed him, you know," I told her. "He was just here."

That brought a moment of bright panic to her. "Johnny?" she said, stiffening in her chair. "He is here?"

"No, he *was* here. About an hour ago. Do you know him?"

Elva was quiet for a moment and then suddenly stood. "I have to go."

"No," I told her. "You don't. You're safe here." I waited as she considered and then sat down again. "Do you know Johnny Caesar?" I asked again.

"*Si*," Elva whispered.

"And you're afraid of him?"

"*Si*," she repeated. Then, in English: "Yes." There was fear in her eyes but there was also a hint of bitter hatred.

"Why?" I asked her. "Why are you afraid?"

Elva took a deep breath, cast a frightened glimpse toward the hallway. "Because *he* killed his *hermano* ..." she said. "His brother."

I blinked. I didn't know what else to do. I didn't know what I expected Elva to say, but I knew I didn't expect this. "Okay, you've got my undivided attention," I said. "Tell me what you know."

Elva opened her mouth, then quickly closed it. She thought a moment, started to speak again, stopped nervously.

"Okay, let me ask the questions," I said. "How do you know the Garcias?"

"I work at Johnny Caesar's building."

KNIFEPOINT

"The August Building." I knew of it. Caesar operated his empire mostly out of his home but, like Tony Soprano, he needed a base of operations to give him some legitimacy. He had purchased a beautiful but aging colonial-style office building in downtown Santa Paula and used most of the top floor there as an office for business he couldn't do at home. The other offices were rented out to legitimate businesses like a real estate manager and a peddler of hotel furniture.

"*Sí,*" Elva continued. "I am a ... how you say? *Portero?*"

"Janitor. Go on."

"*Sí,* a janitor. I work late at night, the ... the cemetery shift ..."

"Graveyard shift."

"The graveyard shift. And Diego, he would come and see me at night and we would talk."

"Talk about what?"

Elva actually smiled a little. "Oh, everything. His brother, his mama, the movies. He liked the *luchadors.*"

The image of Jack Black in a red wrestling mask flashed through my head, "Why am I not surprised?"

Elva raised her eyebrows questioningly.

"It's nothing," I told her. "Please continue."

"Anyway, we talked more and more each night and eventually ... eventually we became more than friends." Elva looked shyly at the floor.

"You were lovers."

119

"*Si,*" she said, without looking up. "Diego was *mi novio.*"

"How long did this go on?"

"About three or four months. Then, one day, we were ... talking ... and Johnny came into the office."

"Late at night?"

"*Si.*"

"He caught you? In the, uh, act?"

"No," Elva said firmly. "We were just talking."

"Okay. And?"

"And he was very angry. He told his brother he did not want him there late at night and he did not want him ..." She bit her lip as she struggled with the word, then said it perfectly. "...fraternizing with the help. He say ..." She stopped again and stared at the floor, this time apparently more ashamed than shy.

"It's okay," I said. "Go on."

"He say, 'Don't shit where you eat.'"

"Smooth talker, that Johnny Caesar. Such a romantic."

That brought a little curl of a smile to Elva's lips. She looked up again and I think she felt just a little more comfortable. "I thought they were going to fight right there, but they did not. They just yelled at each other until, finally, Diego ran out of the building."

"And what did Johnny do?"

"He went to his office and got something. Then he left."

"What'd he get?"

"I did not see."

"Did he say anything to you?"

She shook her head. Her black hair danced delightfully around her delicate features. "No. He just leave."

"When was this?"

"Last Friday night. Or Saturday morning. I get confused."

"I understand. So what makes you think that Johnny killed Diego?"

"Diego told me that Johnny was angry with him for business things. Deals that got ruined that Diego couldn't help. He told me he was scared of his *hermano*."

"When was the last time you talked about this?"

"With Diego? Maybe two weeks ago."

"And a week later he was dead."

A flash of pain shot across her face. Quietly, she mumbled, "Yes."

"I'm sorry," I told her. She nodded silently. "Why did you decide to come to me?"

Elva looked up and I saw in her eyes the genuine pain of someone who has lost someone close. She took a deep, hitching breath. "Because I had no one else to go to," she said at last. Tears welled up in her eyes but, as I reached for a Kleenex on my desk, she shook her head firmly and steadied herself.

"I'm glad you came," I said. "I hope I can help."

"Will you arrest Johnny Caesar?"

"That's not what I do," I told her. "But, if he is responsible for his brother's death, I'll do what I can to be certain that justice is served."

Elva gave me another brave smile and stood up. "Thank you, Mr. Heller."

"Please call me Brace," I told her. I slipped a card out of the holder on my desk and passed it to her. "If you need anything ... or you think of anything more ... please give me a call."

Elva took the card and walked quietly out of my office. As the door closed behind her, I sat down, opened the bottom drawer of the desk, and eyed the Makers Mark. It was only 11:00 now, still too early for a stiff drink. So I walked over to the fridge instead and took out a Coke Zero. I popped it open and took a healthy swig, my body absorbing the carbonation and caffeine like a junky absorbing heroin. It felt good.

Johnny Caesar the guy behind the death of his brother?

Ai Yi Yi.

CHAPTER TWENTY-TWO

Marina peeled another crispy piece of pepperoni off the pizza between us and held it out to me. I leaned forward and took it out of her hand with my lips and ate it. It was wonderfully greasy and absolutely delicious.

"That is *so* bad for you," Marina said.

"Yeah, but it's worth it."

"If you say so." Marina would sooner eat a live rat than a piece of pepperoni. Oh, well. No one's perfect. Not even Marina.

We were on the unmade bed, the pizza box on the sheet between us, only three pieces of pizza left. There would be a grease spot on the sheets where the box soaked through but that, too, would be worth it. Wurzel sat at the foot of the bed, keeping a sharp eye out for any errant scraps that he could pounce on. At least there would be no crumbs in the bed.

I grabbed a Firestone Union Jack from the bed stand and took a long pull. Beer and pizza. Absolute evidence that God exists and that he loves us. Marina took another sip of her homemade margarita. She looked cute there on the bed, in her silk pajamas, eating Toppers' pizza and drinking a margarita from a glass with a stem shaped like cactus.

"So," Marina said, biting the edge of a pizza triangle. "You don't believe this woman?"

"That Johnny killed Diego? No."

"Or had him killed?"

"I don't believe that, either. If Johnny had something to do with Diego's death, why would he want it investigated?"

"To cover his ass?"

"Maybe. But then why come to me? We have a history. He knows I don't like him. He knows that if I discover he's behind it, I'm not going to keep it to myself."

"That's true," Marina said. She picked another piece of pepperoni off of her pizza and fed it to me. "So why would she say he killed his brother?"

"I think she probably believes it," I said. "And, actually, that tells me something. Assuming what she says about her relationship with Diego is true—and there's no reason to believe it isn't—then Johnny and Diego weren't exactly on the best of terms at the time of his death."

"Yeah, but what does that mean?"

I shrugged. "At this point, I don't know. It's just another piece of the puzzle. But it's a piece I didn't have earlier."

Wurzel couldn't take it anymore and rushed me, shoving his cold, wet nose against my cheek and giving me a warm, wet doggy kiss. I wasn't fooled. I knew it was the pepperoni he really loved. So I broke off a little piece and fed it to him.

"That's not good for him, either," Marina said.

"I know."

We ate our pizza silently for a few moments. Pandora, on the iPad on Marina's side, played The Who's "Who Are You?" I wondered when CSI was on next.

Marina took another sip. "So what do you do now?"

"I keep digging," I said. "See what I come up with. If I ask enough questions, talk to enough people, eventually, I'll figure something out."

Marina frowned. "That sounds like it could take a long time."

"It could," I agreed. "Or it could all fall into place tomorrow. That's how it works."

I glanced at the pizza box and realized we'd eaten all the pizza. "What time is CSI on?" I asked.

"It's already over," Marina told me. "Started at nine."

"My little TV Guide." I glanced at the clock on the bed stand. It was 11:15.

Marina closed the empty pizza box and gathered our used napkins. She disappeared for a moment, going into the kitchen to dispose of the trash, and then came back, leaned over the bed and gave me a quick kiss.

"I can't stay tonight," she said. "I've got an early morning meeting."

"Then why are you wearing pajamas?"

"Silk isn't only for sleeping," she purred. And clicked off the bed lamp.

125

CHAPTER TWENTY-THREE

There was a file box, taped up with two-inch shipping tape, sitting in front of my office door when I got there. A bulging manila envelope was perched on top of that. I ignored both for a moment, juggling my Diet Coke while I dug for my keys, and opened the door. I deposited the Coke on my desk and returned for the deliveries, trying not to grunt too much as I lifted them. Never knew who was watching and I couldn't have anyone saying I was a 98-pound weakling.

The box was as heavy as I expected. The return address read "Ventura County Post" and I knew it was filled with old newspaper clippings and photos, courtesy of Andy Larsen.

I carried the box and envelope back and dropped them beside the desk. I glanced briefly at the envelope and put it aside. It was unmarked aside from my name and suite number, but I knew it would be the promo packages for Weapons Grade Charm and, judging from the puffiness, maybe a t-shirt or two. I made a mental note to stop by the Ventura Theater and drop off a package for Destiny.

There was a chill in the air, surprising for a May day.

KNIFEPOINT

The morning sun slanted warmly through the rippled glass window and felt good on my back as I sat down in my desk chair and prepared to do a little newspaper spelunking.

I cut through the shipping tape with the letter opener from my desk and lifted the top of the box away. As expected, it was full of newspaper clippings and photographs, many of which were highlighted here and there in a bright yellow marker. There was a note from Andy on top of the stack.

"Brace: Thanks for this wonderful trip down Memory Lane. I'd forgotten what warm and giving individuals the Garcia Brothers were. Now, if you don't mind, I'm going to go wash my hands with Lava soap. Pumice-Power is really the only thing that will get this filth off. Fuck you very much. Andy."

I smiled and tossed Andy's note in the waste can.

There was really no other way to deal with the stack of paper in the box without just digging in so I did just that. Scooping handfuls of clippings from the box, I stacked them precariously on the desk, preparing for a long, monotonous and probably completely aggravating morning reading about the adventures of the Brothers Garcia. I took a sip of my Diet Coke, thought briefly but seriously about hitting the bottle of Makers Mark in my bottom right drawer, decided it was too early, and then started reading.

You never really forget what scumbags like Johnny

Caesar and his brother are capable of. Their heinous crimes and complete lack of respect for the law speak volumes. But it's easy to push them to the back of your mind, knowing that they're truly bad men but also being aware that there's precious little you can do to stop them.

Still, with the Garcia Brothers' litany of extortion, drug pushing, prostitution, strong-arming, assault and even murder spread set out in black and white columns before me, it didn't take long for that old familiar burn to start coursing through my veins. As I read through their published history, I couldn't help but wonder what unpublished and unpunished crimes they'd committed that didn't appear within these pages. I felt like a complete shit-heel doing anything for these pricks. The money came in handy and the future favor could be important but at that moment, knee deep in their vile world, I wished the opportunity had never arisen.

I read about drug busts and drive-by shootings. I read about vice arrests and arson. I read about a three year old girl who got caught in the crossfire of two rival gangs, one of them Caesar's, and I read about a hooker with an Achilles tendon that had been clipped with wire cutters, and who just also happened to be a client of Marina's.

Because he was the kingpin, most of the shit in the papers was about Johnny. But Diego's name came up often, too. If the Post had a section for "Stupid Criminals," Diego, unlike Johnny, would have been featured there often. He had been popped for a liquor store robbery in Piru but had been released when someone else, another member of Johnny's gang, had stepped forward and claimed responsibility. I was sure that was Johnny's way of saying, "Take the fall, or take the highway," and the highway meant a bullet to the forehead. Diego had been busted time and time again for rifling through parked cars, mostly in his own neighborhood. There were more drug busts than I could keep track of—not many for dealing, but plenty for being under the influence of alcohol, pot or "other." There was the story of the twelve-year-old boy who thought he was protecting his mother when some drug-crazed gangbanger broke into their house. That twelve-year-old boy had received a four inch shiv in the heart for his troubles. There was a brief story about how the police thought they could nail Diego for the crime but it was never mentioned again, at least not in the pages Andy had given me. I knew from my conversation with Powell that the hard evidence was never there and the eyewitnesses who could place Diego in the area had been strangely (but not surprisingly) quiet.

I spent the rest of the morning and part of the afternoon looking through the pages of the Ventura County Post and learning more than I ever wanted to know about the Brothers Garcia. When I finally finished, just before one o'clock, I was ready to pick up the phone and tell Johnny Caesar to fuck off. But it was too late for that now.

I took a one hour break, ran over to the Ventura Theater and dropped off a Weapons Grade Charm promo package for Destiny and then stopped by Bombay for a beer and the salad Marina's voice had shamed me into. I was back in the office by two-fifteen.

As much as I didn't want to, I knew I had to go through the newspaper clippings one more time, this time trying to put aside emotion and focus on facts. The whiskey called to me from the drawer but I ignored it.

At least for now.

CHAPTER TWENTY-FOUR

With the sun beating down hard on the windows of the office, the room had warmed considerably since morning and a deliciously cool breeze was trickling through the window. I could smell the sea salt in the air and it reminded me once again of why I loved living in Ventura.

I had gone through about half of Andy's box again and hadn't found anything I'd missed the first time through. Based on the number of people that the Garcia brothers had wronged and/or conned over the years, I'd been able to limit the number of suspects who'd want to kill Diego to roughly half the population of Santa Paula.

Basically, I was exactly where I started.

The front door suddenly burst open with a much more force than necessary and a second later someone kicked open the office door. Some guy I'd never seen before rushed in, his right arm reaching toward me, some kind of revolver clasped in hand, its blank black eye staring straight at me.

But I had been ready. By the time the guy hit the office door, I'd already pulled the Sig Sauer out of the desk drawer and the moment he took his first step toward me, I was ready to pull the trigger. And did.

With a flash of red spray, the shot caught the intruder in the right bicep and his weapon went flying across the room. The force of the impact knocked the guy to the floor and I was on him with my foot on his throat six seconds after he'd burst into the room.

I looked into his face and confirmed that I'd never seen him before. Whoever he was, he was swarthy, wiry and thin and, if I had to guess, I'd say there was some Greek blood running through him. He wore a pair of grey slacks and a black, long-sleeved turtleneck sweater. His eyes were wild with fury and defeat. His sleeve was soaked with blood, some of which had spilled out onto the floor of my office where it pooled into a pancake-sized puddle.

Kelsey, the woman who ran the temp agency next door, stuck her head in.

"Brace, what ...?" She stopped suddenly as she saw me standing on the guy's throat, and her eyes wandered to the growing slick of blood that stained the tile flooring.

"Call 911," I told her. "Tell them to notify Lieutenant Steven Powell."

Kelsey didn't move.

"Please, Kelsey. Now."

She tore her eyes off the guy on the floor and ran out. I hoped she was off to follow my instructions and not simply get as far away from the violence as possible.

"I got no beef with you," the guy on the floor mumbled. His voice sounded thin and strangled thanks to my heel on his Adam's apple.

"Yeah, that's why you ran in here pointing a gun at me."

"I just wanted to talk business."

"Now might be a good time."

"I want you to stop looking into the Diego Garcia murder."

"Why?"

"I have my reasons."

That wasn't good enough. I dug my foot a little deeper into his throat. "And what might those reasons be?"

"Okay, okay," the guy squeaked. I lifted my foot a bit and he took a few seconds to get his breath. "I was hired to take out Johnny Caesar."

"Oh, so you're the guy. Who hired you?"

"I can't tell you that ..." Again, his voice dwindled to a wheezing gasp as I ground my heel into his Adam's apple.

"This is no time to invoke hitman/client privilege," I said.

His chest heaving, the man on the floor said, "Diego Garcia. His brother."

My conversation with the mysterious Elva came flooding back to me. "Why?"

"Shit, man. He didn't tell me why. He just told me to whack him." He suddenly gasped in pain. "Christ, my arm hurts! You fuckin' shot me!"

"Yes," I told him. "Yes, I did. So if you were hired to kill Johnny Caesar, what the hell are you doing here?"

"I wanted to talk to you."

"Yeah, I could sense that by the way you were firing a gun at my head."

"Nah, I'm serious. I knew you were investigating Diego's murder and I knew it wouldn't be long until the path led to me. If Johnny Caesar finds out who I am and what I was up to, I'm as good as dead. So I was coming here to ask you to leave me out of it."

"You got a strange way of saying 'please,' pal."

"I swear to God, man, I just wanted to talk."

The door burst open again and two uniformed cops crept in, guns drawn. I held up my hands and gently set the Sig Sauer on my desk.

"Guy came in, tried to shoot me with that." I pointed to the 9mm on the floor.

"But you got him first," one of the cops said.

"Used to be a Boy Scout," I said. "Took 'Be Prepared' to heart."

"Whyn't you keep up your hands, just in case."

"All right," I said. "Powell on his way over?"

One of the cops looked at me curiously. "Yeah. Why?"

"He'll vouch for me."

"We'll see."

The other cop knelt by the intruder. "You all right?"

"Nah, man. I'm fuckin' shot."

"Ambulance is on the way. That your gun?"

"Nah, man. I ain't never seen it before."

"I haven't touched it," I said. "You'll find his prints all over it."

"That so?" the cop asked the intruder. The guy didn't respond.

About five minutes later, Powell came sliding through the door. He glanced at the guy on the floor, gave the office a once-over, and then stepped over to me.

"Target practice indoors again? What'd I tell you about that?"

"I didn't think you'd mind," I said, "Seeing as I was almost the target."

"Tell me about it."

We stepped out into the hallway where we wouldn't be overheard and I told him everything. Well, almost everything. I told him how the guy had burst in, ready to shoot. I told him everything the guy had told me, including the fact that he had been hired to take out Johnny Caesar. For now, I left Elva out of it. The shooter didn't seem to know about her and there didn't seem to be any reason to involve her. At least at this point.

The paramedics came, pushed past us, and started bandaging the shooter up.

"So Johnny Caesar had a contract out on him, huh?" Powell said. "And you didn't think to tell me."

"Hell, I didn't know until last night," I said. "Caesar seemed to think that was unrelated to what he hired me for."

"What about you?"

135

"I'm not so sure. This guy says Diego hired him to kill Johnny. If that's the case, and we have no reason to believe it's not, then there's no way Mr. Killer here mistook Diego for his brother."

"Yeah, that's what I'm thinkin'."

The paramedics wheeled their gurney past us. The wannabe hitman glared at me as he went by. I might have shivered in fear except that I knew Powell was there to protect me.

"Keep an eye on him," Powell told the two cops, who followed the paramedics into the hall toward the elevator. "I don't want him going anywhere." He turned back to me. "So where does this leave you?" Powell asked.

I shook my head in disgust. "Back at square frigging one," I said.

CHAPTER TWENTY-FIVE

Powell stayed for a while and had a Coke Zero. I opted for half a shot of Makers Mark. He said he just wanted to stay for a moment to shoot the breeze, but I knew he was really making sure I was all right. Even we badasses get a little jittery when someone tries to put a bullet in us. But my hand wasn't shaking as I passed him a can of Coke and I knew that would make him feel better. It made me feel better, too.

Powell finished his soda at a leisurely pace and then stood. He told me to stay out of trouble and said goodbye. No sooner had the door closed behind him when the phone rang. I glanced at my watch. 6:15. Past normal business hours, but, hey, I was still here in the office and it might be Marina wondering why I was late.

"Heller Investigations."

"Brace, it's Destiny, over at the Ventura Theater."

"Hey, Destiny. What's up? You get a chance to listen to my guys?"

"Yeah, that's why I'm calling. This is a great band you found, Brace."

"I think so, too."

"They as good live as they are on the CD?"

"Better. The best bands always are."

"Agreed. Yeah, these guys are great. I think they might be the ones you've been looking for."

I thought, *From your lips to God's ears*, but I didn't say it.

"So," I said, "You gonna give them the opening slot for Tommy Hogart?"

There was a pause on the other end and I felt my heart sink. Then, Destiny said, "You know what, Brace? I'm going to give them *an* opening slot. I've got three slots to fill and I'll give your boys one of them. They may not be the band just before Tommy, but they'll get their shot. Will that work for you?"

"That'll work just fine, Destiny."

"I'll give them half an hour in either the number one or two slot."

"Number two would be better."

"I know. Do what I can."

"Thanks."

"Hey, thank *you* for bringing them to me.

"Anything for a free ticket."

Destiny laughed. "We're gonna have a great show that night. Tell your guys to be here at three for rehearsal and soundcheck, all right?"

"You got it. Thanks again."

"Have a good one, Brace"

I dropped the phone back into the cradle. *Weapons Grade Charm* opening for Tommy Hogart.

Ya-freaking-hoo!

138

CHAPTER TWENTY-SIX

I couldn't wait to tell the members of Weapons Grade Charm that they had scored an opening slot for Tommy Hogart, so I grabbed my coat, locked up shop and high-tailed it over to their rehearsal space on California.

No one was there. The place was dark and, in fact, there was a shiny new chain looped through the doors. I wondered if the band had been caught in the midst of one of their illegal rehearsals and told to hit the highway. I hoped they'd remember to call me and tell me where they were going to rehearse now.

On a whim, I walked down the street to the Sans Souci and good fortune followed me. There, sitting at the bar, brown bottles and empty shot glasses in front of them, were the four members of *Weapons Grade Charm*.

"Gentlemen!"

"Hey, Brace!" Keith Guillotine said, hopping off his barstool and shaking my hand firmly. He seemed genuinely glad to see me. Either that, or he'd done a few shots already. "We got locked out of our rehearsal space."

"Yeah, I saw that. Did you get your equipment out, at least?"

"Yeah, the guy wasn't an asshole about it or anything," Guillotine said. "He just said that we couldn't play there because of insurance and gave us a few minutes to clean out all our stuff."

"We offered him a beer," said JD2, his enormous beard quivering like a mass of stainless steel wool. "But he said it would cost more than one beer for the rent!"

JD2 laughed hysterically while the rest of us just stared. Apparently, he was his own best audience.

I turned my attention to the bartender. "Hey, Shell. Round of whiskey for us. Makers Mark, please."

Shell raised her eyebrows hopefully. "Me, too?"

"You bet."

Shell pulled the bottle from the shelf behind her and poured six neat shots. She passed one to each of the band members and one to me. The only other person in the bar, a drunk huddled in the corner, looked up at me thirstily so I gave Shell the okay to pour him a shot, too.

We all raised our glasses (except the drunk, who had already downed his shot by the time we lifted ours) and I said, "To *Weapons Grade Charm*, who are opening for Tommy Hogart right across the street at the Ventura Theater."

I drained my shot as did Shell and JD2. The others just stared.

"We got it?" Saint Snider finally asked.

"You got it," I confirmed. "Talked to Destiny today. She loved the package and can't wait to see you guys live."

Saint Snider smiled and guzzled his whiskey. "Fuckin' A!" he said, slamming the shot glass down on the bar. JD1 quickly followed suit.

Keith Guillotine was still staring at me. "We're opening for Tommy Hogart?" he asked quietly.

"Yes, you are," I told him. "You won't get the slot just before the headliner, but you're on the bill. I'm hoping you'll get the second spot, there'll be more people in the audience then, but even the first opening slot is a score."

"That's *awesome*," Guillotine said. He tipped his shot glass to his lips, drained whatever vestiges of Makers Mark were left there.

"Hey, it's not like it's Woodstock," I said. "But it's a nice start. You'll get some good local publicity out of it, maybe a little buzz. Get people talking about you on social media."

Guillotine dropped his glass on the bar and stretched an open palm toward me. I took his hand and shook it.

"Thanks, Brace. You did it. You came through for us."

"Don't go buying a house in Malibu," I said. "This is less than a baby step. If you're the first band of the evening, the house will only be a quarter or so full."

Saint Snider squinted at me. "Then why bother playing at all?"

Guillotine slapped him on the arm. "Because we've been trying to get an opening gig there for six months and haven't even got a call back."

"Yeah, but a quarter full? What is that? A hundred people?"

"More like three hundred, if you're lucky," I said. "But what's the biggest audience you've played to so far?"

Saint Snider nodded. "About forty. At the Red Cove. On New Year's eve."

Guillotine scoffed. "More like twenty."

"Okay, and you were playing to an audience that was more about getting their drink on than listening to a new band," I said. "The audience at the Ventura Theater, especially the ones who are there early, will be there for the music."

JD1 said, "That makes sense."

"Plus," I continued. "You don't *want* to be the band that plays just before Tommy. That can be a thankless spot. The audience is all revved up and rarin' to go, but they're getting less and less patient for the headliner to start. Unless you're damn good and well known..."

"We are damn good," Saint Snider said.

"Yeah, but you're not well known. You'll be heckled throughout your set. Do you really want people chanting 'Tommy! Tommy! Tommy!' when you've still got two more songs to play?"

Saint Snider shook his head.

"So, I think this is a great place to start." I slapped Saint Snider on the shoulder, turned to Shell and pointed at the whiskey bottle. "Let's do that again, Shell, whattya say?"

Shell smiled. "I say yes."

There was a Post-It with a note from Marina stuck to the answering machine when I got home asking me to call her at her place. So I did.

"You're home late," she said.

"One of those days," I told her. "Like you wouldn't believe."

"So, tell me about it."

So I told her about it.

"Poor baby," Marina said, after a short pause, when I had finished telling her about my guest with the gun. "At least he didn't put a hole in that lovely head of yours." I knew her non-chalance about the situation was her way of dealing with it. I also knew it was as much for me as it was for her.

"But there is some good news," I said. "Destiny gave *Weapons Grade Charm* an opening slot for Tommy Hogart."

"That *is* good news!"

"Well, *one* of the opening slots," I clarified. "It's a four band line-up and they're going to get the first or second position."

"Well, that's still great, isn't it?"

"It's a start," I said. "Now, if I can get some reviewers out there and drum up some good press, we'll be on a roll."

"What about that guy at RoughEdge.com?" Marina asked. "They still operate out of Ventura, don't they?"

"That's a good idea," I said. "I'll give him a call. They're usually more than willing to cover local bands."

We talked for a while about mostly nothing and then quietly rang off. I looked at the clock. It was now 11:30pm. I could watch one of the two Jimmys—Kimmel or Fallon—or switch back and forth between them, depending on how strong their guests were. Or I could just go to bed.

It was much easier just to go to bed.

At 2:47 AM the phone woke me out of a mild nightmare in which I had fallen into the ocean when surfing and got tangled up in a mass of seaweeds. The seaweeds were clutching at me, pulling me and I couldn't make my way to the surface.

The phone's shrill ring made the bad seaweeds vanish instantly.

"Heller," I said into the phone.

"Brace, it's Powell." His voice was low and quiet. I knew something was dreadfully wrong.

"What is it, Steve?" I asked.

"It's your friend, Kristyn, over at O'Leary's," Powell said. "She's dead."

CHAPTER TWENTY-SEVEN

With a heavy heart, a painful hollowness in my chest, and only a scythe of moon glowing half-heartedly in the early morning sky, the drive over to O'Leary's seemed darker than normal, almost black. The night was still and supernaturally quiet. As I cruised past the Government Center on Telephone Road, I could see the wash of red lights flashing in the parking lot at O'Leary's.

The first thing I noticed as I pulled into the lot was a chaotic conglomeration of black-and-white police cars and beige undercover vehicles. They were parked every which way, many of them with the doors wide open, their occupants standing about, some talking animatedly, others just standing and watching with grim faces. The second thing I noticed was the body, covered with a white sheet, lying in the middle of the parking lot, the lake of blood beneath it shimmering in the flashing red lights. Powell and a pair of uniforms I didn't know stood talking beside it, their faces masks of serious intent. I felt that hollowness in my chest grow as I faced the reality of it all.

I parked the Camry near a black-and-white and told the cop leaning against it I was there to see Powell, who had phoned for me. The cop didn't know me from Adam but apparently figured I knew the right names so he waved me past.

"Brace, Jesus, sorry to call you with this," Powell said as I approached. "I know you two were close."

"What happened?"

"Near as we can tell, he was waiting for her when she left the building. Cold-cocked her friend over there ..." He pointed to a short brick wall where a young man with a blanket around his shoulders sat, a cold compress on his forehead, paramedics giving him the once-over. "... And then stabbed her to death. We figure, fourteen, fifteen wounds."

"Motherfucker," I hissed.

"Murder weapon's over there," Powell said, pointing. "We don't know if the perp tossed it or simply lost it as he ran to his car."

I followed the direction of Powell's pointing finger and saw a knife laying there in the rolling red neon glow. I'd seen that type of knife before. It was the same brand and model I'd found when Kristen had called me before and the same kind of knife I'd seen at Ian Kilgore's home.

The bastard must have bought them wholesale.

I knelt by the body and reached out to pull back the sheet. I didn't want to see Kristyn like this, but I had to. I felt responsible for putting her there. I had thought I could scare Kilgore away from her with a simple but heartfelt threat and now, too late, I realized it would require much more than that. I felt the words "I'm sorry,"

146

slip past my lips in a silent whisper as I reached for the corner of the sheet and pulled it away from the corpse's face.

Her eyes were closed, probably by Powell or someone else early on the scene. Even in this light, they seemed forced and unnatural. Except for the eyes, her face still had a look of terror on it, as though frozen there as the knife descended again and again. Blonde hair spilled onto the pavement in a wavy cascade and where it touched the ground, it was soaked in a pool of sticky, black blood. Her body was twisted in an unnatural way that told me she was probably fatally wounded before she hit the ground.

I stood up, took a deep breath, and turned to Powell. "That's not Kristyn," I said.

Powell looked at me in surprise. "You're sure?"

"Yeah, I'm sure. I've known her since she was a kid. That's not her. Didn't you talk to her escort yet?"

"Not yet. He took a bump on the head and he's pretty shook up." He turned to one of the uniforms beside him. "Jimmy, go ask the witness what her name is." Jimmy ran off to comply.

"Well, this isn't Kristyn," I said, feeling a wave of relief wash through me, a wave that did nothing to diminish my burning rage. "But, whoever it is, Kilgore did it. That's his knife over there. I've seen it at his home."

"He was my first thought," Powell said. "I've sent a car over to his place to collect him."

147

"Should have sent me."

"I would have liked to," Powell said. He touched his bottom lip with his pen and added, "If this isn't Kristyn, who is it?"

"Don't know."

"Where's Kristyn?"

"I told her to take a few days off work," I said. "Last I heard, she was staying at her mother's. I'll drop by and make sure everything's all right."

I turned and headed to the car.

"Brace," Powell called after me.

I stopped, turned. "Yeah?"

"Stay away from Kilgore's place," he said. "Let us handle this."

I nodded grimly and turned away.

Kristyn was at her mother's house on the Avenue and, when I told her what had happened, she immediately burst into tears. Heaving and sobbing, she told me that she had asked Robin, a co-worker, to cover for her, and that she had never even thought about the fact that they looked vaguely alike. I told her that she had done nothing wrong and that there was nothing she could have done differently. I told her the blame was all Kilgore's and only he was responsible. I held her on the front porch for a while and we talked quietly. Occasionally, she started sobbing again and I would try to comfort her. Finally, when a neighbor complained about the noise and I threatened to shoot out their porch light, Kristyn gave me a little smile and said she was all right. She went back inside, hopefully to sleep. But I knew it would be a fitful sleep, if it ever came.

Then I went to Ian Kilgore's house.

Kilgore's big Caddie wasn't in front of his house but a black-and-white was. I introduced myself to the two uniforms who were there and they told me they'd been there since Powell sent them over right after he'd arrived at O'Leary's. They hadn't seen hide nor hair of Kilgore since they arrived.

"You go in?" I asked.

"Not yet," they said. "Knocked on the door is all. Nobody answered. Powell didn't give us the go-ahead to go in."

I wished them a good night and good hunting and drove the Camry around the block to where I had parked it just a few nights before. I went through the backyards again, more quietly this time since I knew where the gates were, and let myself in Kilgore's back door. The haft was still broken and the door swung open easily.

As the uniforms had told me, Kilgore wasn't home. He had killed Robin and then took off, God only knew where. I pulled out my penlight and began searching the apartment. Maybe there was a clue here that would tell me where he was hiding. Maybe I'd find something more to tie him to the murder. Maybe the son of a bitch would come home and I could put a hot slug into his demented brain.

I was careful not to let the light near the window and tip off the two cops outside that I was in here. Last thing I needed was for them to come bursting in, thinking I was Kilgore. But I searched the place from top to bottom: drawers, under the bed, inside the refrigerator, everywhere. As always seemed to be the case, however, I found what I was looking for sitting in plain sight in an ashtray on the kitchen counter.

It was a matchbook from the Gila Motel on Main Street. I slipped it into my pocket and let myself out the back door.

I didn't bother closing it behind me.

The Gila Motel was a rundown shack of a motel, shaped like a square-edged U with only one entrance. There were twelve rooms inside—five on the left, five on the right and two in the back—and I knew from past experience that most of them contained druggies and partiers who just wanted to go somewhere that was cheap where they could get high in peace.

But the big Cadillac Fleetwood parked in the darkness beneath a stretch of eucalyptus trees told me that someone else was there, as well.

I parked on Main Street and walked to the Gila's office. The door was locked but I could see the clerk leaning way back in his tattered chair, sound asleep. When traffic wasn't passing, I could hear the rasp of his snore. I leaned on the buzzer until he came to and waited patiently while he took his sweet time getting to the window. He slid back the Plexiglass divider angrily.

"The fuck you want?" he growled.

"Great customer service technique," I said. "I bet you're employee of the month every month, aren't you? Which room is the guy with the Caddie in?"

The clerk leaned forward and peered down toward the eucalyptus trees. "Can't tell you that," he said with a wry smile. "Customer privacy." He pushed his palm fingers into silver tray beneath the window and wiggled his fingers. Customer privacy obviously had a price.

I grabbed his wrist and gave it a hard tug.

"Hey! What the fu..."

That sentence came to an abrupt halt as the clerk's head thunked against the glass, leaving a greasy, amoeba-like smudge, and he gave out a frightened mewl. Fluorescent lighting sparkled off the fresh blood exposed where the skin of his knuckles had pulled back when I had yanked them through the payment tray. His face was pressed comically against the window but I was betting he didn't think it was funny.

"Which room?" I asked again.

"Fuck, man, let go of me."

"Which room?"

"Nine. He's in room nine."

I glanced down at nine. It was in the far right hand corner. The lights were off. Looked quiet.

"You sure?"

"Yeah, yeah, I'm sure. Fuck, man. Let go of my hand."

I let go of his hand. "Go back to sleep," I said. "Stay off the phone."

Rubbing his injured hand, the clerk only nodded at me with wide eyes. I saw real fear there and I didn't think he'd call the cops. Yet. There was something else in his eyes, too. A kind of morbid curiosity. He wanted to see what happened next and he hoped it was bloody.

He was probably going to get his wish.

I gave him a warning glare and then headed toward room number nine.

I walked right past it at first and then around to the back. These places were old school. There were small patios around back, with big sliding glass doors, and a wrought iron fence surrounding them. But, with the railroad running no more than fifty feet away and a big scrap metal yard the only thing you could see on the other side of the tracks, no one used the patios much anymore. Instead, they were used to store unwanted shit left behind by renters: rusty barbecue grills, broken bicycles and soggy couches.

There were no lights on inside Kilgore's room and I could detect no hint of movement. He was probably hiding in bed again, feigning sleep, and clutching another one of those vicious hunting knifes in his cowardly grasp.

KNIFEPOINT

I walked back around to the front door of Number 9, staying well clear of the window, and leaned silently against the door. I gave the door knob a slow, careful turn. Locked. I glanced back at the office. The lights were out and the blinds were closed and I was sure the clerk was watching me through the blinds. Let him watch. My guess was he was looking for a cheap thrill rather than a reason to call the police.

I leaned a little harder on the door and heard it creak. It felt flimsy and old. I figured I could bust it down and be on Kilgore in about two seconds.

A sudden, muffled pop made me flinch and a slug ripped through the door just inches from my head. Tiny splinters bit into my face as I dropped to my knees and fell against the door jamb. Another slug ripped through the cheap wood just above me. I could sense lights flipping on throughout the complex behind me.

Kilgore was aiming high, not realizing I had dropped to my knees, and—before he could correct his mistake—I crushed my shoulder hard into the door. It went as easily as I thought it would and, in the flare of another shot (something whistled by too close to my right ear), I saw Kilgore standing near his bed, wearing only a pair of boxers and holding a gun in his right hand. I made right for him, slamming my shoulder into his midriff before he could pull the trigger again. The force of the impact took Kilgore by surprise and he lost the gun. It clattered to the floor somewhere beside me.

153

We fell on the filthy carpet in a tangle and Kilgore was beating at me wildly. His fists fell with little impact but he was fired up and terrified and he rained blows upon me in a surprisingly steady succession. I tried to push him away but his fists found my face and, although they did little damage, it was enough to keep me disconcerted for a split second.

Kilgore twisted away and rolled toward his gun. I rolled with him and gave a little yelp as something dug into my ribcage. I snatched it away and glanced at it just for a second.

It was one of Kilgore's hunting knives. Closed and discarded on the floor.

Kilgore scrabbled to the wall and grabbed the gun. He turned with it just as I flipped open the knife. His finger was just snaking around the trigger when I rammed the blade deep into his wrist. I couldn't see in the darkness of the room, but it felt like it had gone in one side and right out the other.

Kilgore cried out in shock and pain as the gun practically jumped out of his hands and flew across the room. I grabbed hold of the knife handle and rammed the blade into the nearest wall. Luck was with me and I hit drywall and not a stud. The drywall was old but still firm and the knife stuck tightly; Kilgore flailed but couldn't pull his arm free from the wall. Each attempt made him scream in ragged agony and finally he gave up, slumped to the floor, defeated.

154

KNIFEPOINT

He was bleeding badly. I hoped that I had hit an artery.

I pushed myself away, pulled the Sig Sauer from its holster, and pointed it at Kilgore's face. "If you move, I will kill you," I told him plainly. He apparently saw the seriousness in my eyes and his body went limp.

With my other hand, I fumbled my cellphone out of my pocket and dialed Powell's cell. When he answered, I told him where I was and he said, "Oh, Christ, that's you? We're on our way."

I sat on the sagging bed, the gun still pointed at Kilgore, and stared at him, hanging there from the wall. He was sobbing in choked little bursts but I couldn't tell if it was from pain or the frustration of being caught.

"You stupid shit," I told him. "Not only do you ignore my warning, you go out and kill the wrong girl."

Kilgore looked up at me then, shocked puzzlement in his eyes, and then looked quickly away.

"Yeah, that's right," I told him. "Kristyn's fine. You killed her friend, you stupid bastard."

Kilgore gave another mewl of pain and frustrated rage and I just sneered at him. "The cops are on the way," I told him. "Lucky for you."

CHAPTER TWENTY-EIGHT

Powell gave me a loud and convincing reprimand in front of his people.

"What the hell were you thinking?"

"Let the police do their job!"

"I could run you in for this!"

After a few withering moments, he led me over to the Camry and asked quietly, "How'd you know he was here?"

"I didn't," I said. "It was just a hunch."

"Pretty good fuckin' hunch."

"That's all it was."

"Whatever. Worked out okay. Saved us all some time and money."

"Glad to be of service."

Powell scowled. "Did you go see your friend?"

"Yeah. She's taking it all pretty hard. Blaming herself."

"This wasn't her fault."

"I know. Try telling her that."

Powell nodded. "Listen, we'll have to do a report tomorrow. Standard bullshit. Nothing to worry about."

"I understand."

KNIFEPOINT

Powell stared at me a moment longer and said, "Christ, man, you look like shit. Why don't you go home and get some sleep."

"I will. See you tomorrow."

"Yeah. I'll call you."

The ebony sky was just starting to show the first signs of the dawning day when I walked back into the house. Wurzel, stretched out on his pillowy bed on the floor, lifted his head lazily, made sure it was me and not some delicious burglar, and then promptly put his head back down and went instantly to sleep.

My body ached everywhere, especially in the spots where Kilgore's rain of sickly blows had found their mark. I wanted nothing more than a few hours shuteye but knew that wasn't going to happen. I was too keyed up and needed at least few minutes to wind down. I opened the freezer, cracked out a couple of ice cubes, dropped them into a highball glass and poured a shot of Makers Mark over them. It wasn't my favorite way to drink whiskey but I wasn't in the mood for a room temperature shot at the moment.

I sipped my whiskey, mused about all the things I needed to do today and waited until my eyelids were too heavy to keep open.

It didn't take long.

CHAPTER TWENTY-NINE

It was one of those warm, beautiful days that reminded me why I'd lived in Ventura my entire life. *Crystal* seemed a good word to describe it. Only a few tiny cloud puffs clung stubbornly to the bright and soothing blue of the morning sky. The sun beamed pleasantly through the window of the Camry as I drove, toasting the cabin with its golden rays. The world seemed vivid, clean and full of joy.

Me, not so much. Due to lack of sleep and the early morning stress of dealing with a certain Mr. Kilgore (as well as the couple of whiskeys I'd downed before falling asleep), I felt gritty and listless. My brain seemed to be resting in a pan full of sand and my sore joints didn't want to flex. I made a mental note to get to bed early tonight but knew that I wouldn't. Something else would crop up. It always does.

I guided the Camry over to police headquarters and met Powell there. He sat me down with some grumpy desk jockey who took my report with a lack of interest that was monumental. We were done in twenty minutes or so and I was back on the road to Santa Paula. It was just past 11 o'clock.

KNIFEPOINT

I took the 126 freeway all the way out to the South 10th Street off-ramp, just a few miles before Santa Paula becomes Fillmore. I drove past Harvard Boulevard—the street Diego Garcia had died on—and took 10th Street up a few blocks until I came to The August Building. I parked on the street opposite the building, thankful that Santa Paula, unlike Ventura, had yet to put parking meters there, and I settled back for what would probably be a boring and fruitless afternoon.

Elva's visit to my office yesterday had piqued my curiosity. She had claimed to have cared for Diego, and had proved that much by coming to see me. However, her fear of Johnny Caesar seemed to outweigh any feelings she had for his brother. She told me she was a janitor, and that she worked the graveyard shift, so the odds of my running into her at this time of day were slim. That was a good thing. She was scared enough as it was. If she saw me snooping around her place of employment, she'd probably never have the courage to speak to me again. Or, worse, she might draw attention to herself by acting oddly and then catch Johnny's attention, something she definitely didn't want to do.

I kept running over her story in my mind. What was that friction between Diego and his brother? Was it a power play? Was it simple sibling rivalry? Had Johnny told Diego he had had enough of his trouble-making and threatened to cut him out of the family? Had Diego decided that Johnny had played king of the hill long enough, and it was time to give somebody else a chance? Or was it something else entirely.

Indeed, was there something at all? The fact of the matter is that I didn't know if Elva was lying, or perhaps just mistaken about what she'd seen.

I sat in the car, windows down, watching the front door of the August Building. Metallica's black album played low on the stereo. The three Breakfast Jacks I'd bought that morning eventually disappeared, each one colder than the one that preceded it. I was out of Diet Coke; the ice rattled around in the plastic cup anxiously, as though in fear of its unavoidable transformation back to water.

A few non-descript people entered and exited the August Building, probably trying to sell something or just going about their day's business. They were absolutely no help to me and probably the better for not realizing it. The day grew warmer as the sun climbed higher. Sweat oozed through the back of my shirt and glued me to the driver's seat. My ass grew numb on the lumpy cloth seat cushion. Stake-outs were never much fun and this one, which really had no point except trying to kickstart my disinterested mind, ranked as one of the worst.

A homeless man stumbled up to my window and asked me for a dollar. I gave him the twenty-eight cents that was in my ash tray. He grumbled a half-hearted thanks and wandered aimlessly away.

At about 12:30pm, the front doors opened and my

client, none other than Johnny Caesar himself, stepped out into the glaring sunlight. He slipped on a pair of Ray Ban shades and stood at the curb with his arms crossed, waiting. A moment later, she joined him.

She was a beautiful Latino woman, her abundant hair cascading down past her shoulders in voluptuous waves of glimmering black. She wore a pair of large, round, designer sunglasses, a breathtakingly short black skirt, a matching jacket and a white top, open at the neck probably two buttons more than it should have been. Not that I was complaining. The ridiculous high heels she wore gave her an extra three inches height which, judging from where I was sitting, made her well-conditioned body seem perfect in almost every perspective.

I didn't know who she was but I knew this much: She wasn't Johnny Caesar's wife, who was an attractive woman herself but years older and considerably doughier than this woman.

Johnny, you old dog, I thought.

A black Town Car pulled up and, before the driver could hop out and grab the doors for them, Johnny had opened the door on his own, allowed his dark-haired beauty to slip in before him, and then climbed into the backseat. The driver quickly jumped back into the car and a moment later, it pulled into traffic and headed south.

I waited until the Town Car turned right at the next corner and then started the Camry and spun a quick U-turn. I turned right at the same corner and was just in time to see the Town Car turn right again, two streets ahead of me, on North Mill Street.

I stepped on the gas as the Town Car disappeared from view, and then turned at the same corner it had. I was shocked and disappointed to see that the Town Car had vanished. Either it had already made the next corner and turned right or left—in which case I had only had a 50/50 shot at guessing correctly—or it had pulled into a parking lot somewhere off the street.

I continued down North Mill and was rewarded with a glimpse to my left of Johnny and his mystery date climbing out of the Town Car in the parking lot of the Glen Tavern Inn. The Inn was a quaint and romantic hotel that became a Federal historical landmark in 1984. It was built in 1911 and throughout the years has served as a gambling center, a house of ill repute and a speak-easy.

I watched Johnny and the girl walk through the ho-tel's front door and, although my mind started musing salaciously, I knew that the Glen Tavern Inn was also the home of Enzo's Italian Restaurant, one of Marina's favorite places to eat. So it was either fornication or mastication that Johnny and his friend had in mind and, without even knowing why, I decided I should probably find out which.

I cruised casually past the Inn, turned right, and parked the car on East Santa Barbara Street. It took me about three minutes to walk back to the Inn, and by then the Town Car was gone. I was hoping that the driver had just gone off to run some errands while his passengers did their thing and that I hadn't missed them.

If Johnny and his lunch date were still inside, it would be risky going into the lobby—there was no way to be certain that I wouldn't walk right smack dab into them— but I didn't have any choice. I needed to know whether they were headed to the registration desk or the restaurant and that was the only way I was going to find out. So in I went.

The lobby of the Glen Tavern Inn was cozy, regal and nostalgic all at once. It was more of a parlor than a lobby, complete with rich, comfortable sofas and tables with reading lights. You could imagine being a guest there and actually spending time in the lobby, reading your morning newspaper and enjoying a piping hot cup of coffee. It truly did seem like a home away from home.

And, thankfully, it was also virtually empty at the moment. Except for a grinning registration clerk whose friendly smile was almost preternaturally warm, I was the only person enjoying the room's ambiance.

"Good afternoon, sir," said the clerk happily, tossing her long, brown hair over her shoulder. "How can I help you today?"

"I'm looking for a friend," I told her, which was half true. I *was* looking for someone but he was anything but a friend.

"In the restaurant?" the clerk asked.

163

"I believe so," I told her. "I'll take a look. If he's not there, I'll wait at the bar. I'm sure he'll be along shortly."

"That'll be fine," she said, lighting up that smile again. "Have a nice day, sir."

"You do the same."

The entrance to Enzo's was inside the lobby, just to the left of the registration desk. I walked casually to the entrance. Before the Maitre'd had time to greet me, I quickly and quietly said, "Just here for a drink" and headed over to the completely empty bar.

I sat on the second stool from the end, close enough that I could scan virtually every table in the restaurant, but far enough away so that I couldn't easily be seen myself.

The lunch crowd was just starting to thin out but the restaurant was still more than half full. I scanned the diners, looking for a familiar face, and was just about to give up when I found them.

Johnny Caesar and his voluptuous friend were tucked into a cozy little corner, sitting at a small, dark table near the back of the room. Away from the windows, I noticed. A carafe of red wine sat on the table in front of them. They faced each other and chatted quietly, exactly like clandestine lovers trying to maintain the secrecy of their relationship. But, although their body language and facial expressions indicated they were infatuated with one another, there was no physical contact. They didn't hold hands, didn't stroke one another's hair, and never came

164

close to kissing. Either they weren't romantically linked after all or they were better than average at hiding it.

"Good afternoon, sir. What can I get ya?"

The beefy bartender had slipped up on me unexpectedly and, for a moment, I felt like a kid caught with his hand in the cookie jar.

Or maybe a peeper caught peering into a window.

"Got anything local on tap?"

"Topa Topa. We've got their Level Line Pale Ale, their Sespe Pils and their Chief Peak IPA."

"Chief Peak. Perfect. Thanks."

"You got it. Like to see a menu?"

"Sure."

As the bartender went off to pour my beer, I glanced back over at Johnny to see that a server had approached them and had given them menus. They pored through them eagerly, chatting about the choices and laughing gaily.

My Chief Peak was delivered and I took an ice cold sip. It was outstanding, one of my favorite local beers. The bitterness bristled delightfully across my tongue.

The bartender slid a menu over to me. "Lunch is on the inside cover," he said.

I glanced over at Johnny's table. They still had their noses in the menu, enthusiastically discussing which item to order. I knew what I would recommend.

"On second thought, I don't need a menu," I told the bartender. "I'll have the *Pollo al Limone*."

The bartender nodded, impressed. "A regular, I see."

"Regular might be overdoing it," I told him. "But I do love the food here."

I sat there for nearly an hour, ordered another beer and relished my deliciously tangy *Pollo al Limone*. Johnny and his date happily enjoyed their lunch across the restaurant from me. From where I sat, it looked as though he ordered lasagna, she (predictably) a salad. Throughout the meal, they chatted happily, laughed a lot and occasionally clinked their wineglasses together cheerfully. But not a trace of what the tabloids call PDA.

I finished my lunch and had another beer, switching from the hoppy, deliciously bitter Chief Peak to the smoother taste of the Sespe Pils. It wasn't as hearty as the Chief Peak but it was cold and refreshing nonetheless.

Finally, the server cleared away the last of the dishes from Johnny's table and he and his date stood. I watched her as she stretched her feline form, uncoiling from the cozy booth after a leisurely lunch, while Johnny not so clandestinely enjoyed the view. She caught him looking and took his hands in hers, stood up on her tip-toes and gave him a not-so-platonic kiss, her tongue darting in between his lips. Johnny stiffened, and pushed her gently but firmly away, glancing around at the other diners nervously.

Bingo.

I was careful to turn my head away as they left the restaurant, and I watched their backs as they faded into the lobby. I watched with electric anticipation as they walked toward the front desk. Which way would they turn? Right toward the front doors or left toward the guest rooms? I held my breath as they stepped into the lobby area, paused for a moment...

...and then headed up the stairs to the guest rooms.

Bingo again!

This wasn't just a lunch date, but a lunch date with benefits.

I sat at the bar and fiddled with my phone for a while, occasionally glancing over at the stairway to see if Johnny and his friend had changed their minds and came back downstairs. After about twenty minutes, I decided they were in for the long haul so I paid the server and left the Inn. It was almost three o'clock and I was anxious to get home, take some notes and think about what I had just witnessed. I walked back to the Camry and had just opened the door when my phone rang. I recognized Keith Guillotine's number and made a mental note to add him to the phone's address book.

"Hey, Keith," I said. "Heller."

"Hey, Brace," Guillotine said, and I immediately sensed the tension in his tone. "We're not going to be able to play that fucking show."

CHAPTER THIRTY

I fell into the drivers' seat, closed my eyes and hung my head. Guillotine's agitated voice buzzed angrily in my ear. Apparently, *Weapons Grade Charm* had met for rehearsal that afternoon and tempers had flared over songwriting credit. Swell. Just how I wanted to end my day: Spend the next six hours babysitting a bunch of whiny musicians.

"I wrote that song like three years ago," Guillotine was screaming. "And he wants co-writing credit because his guitar solo is in it."

Yada yada yada.

I let him go on for a while and then gently told him to shut the hell up. "Get everyone together," I told him, "And meet me at my office in twenty minutes." Guillotine started to protest. "Just do it," I said firmly. And hung up. Either they showed or they didn't. If they did, I'd help them solve their problem. If they didn't, I could always tear up that management agreement and get out while the getting was good.

I turned the ignition key and the little Toyota engine buzzed to life, eager to take me wherever I wanted to go next. I wanted to go home, kick back in my Lazy Boy and watch some mindless TV but, thanks to the egos of four wanna-be rock stars, I was on my way back to my office.

Which is one of the reasons I kept the refrigerator there fully stocked with alcohol at all times.

I paid for parking on California Street and took the stairs up to my office. The elevator was notoriously slow and creaky and sometimes wasn't worth the wait.

The members of *Weapons Grade Charm* were already there, leaning against the wall and sitting on the floor as though posing for an album cover. Nobody said a word as I unlocked the office door and we all stepped inside.

"Grab a chair," I told them, and headed for the fridge. It took me a second to decide—Union Jack or Torpedo?—but I went with the slightly smoother Union Jack. "Get yourselves a beer," I told the others. "But not the Bigfoot Barleywine, that's mine." To the last man, they each grabbed a beer—depleting my supply of both Union Jack *and* Torpedo—and fell into the client chairs scattered around the office. Bottlecaps were popped; beer was sipped, silence ensued.

"Okay," I said after a moment. "Who wants to start?"

Saint Snider opened his mouth to speak but Guillotine cut him off, exploding into yet another version of the same conversation he'd started with me half an hour earlier. Saint Snider listened for a few seconds and then started bleating his own version of the situation. JD1 and JD2 sat idly, both of them, I'm certain, figuring this wasn't their battle and wanting to stay the hell out of it.

The grating, ever-louder chaos annoyed me. "Wait,

wait, *wait!*" I said loudly, holding up my palm. "One at a time, goddammit, I can't understand a word." I shot my finger at Guillotine. "You," I said. "Go."

"Okay, it's like this," Guillotine started. "I wrote this song, 'Warm in Winter,' before I even joined this band, like six years ago. I brought it to the band like three years ago and we've played it in our set ever since. Now, all of the sudden, he wants writing credit, even though it's *my* song."

I held up my hand like a traffic cop, then pointed at Saint Snider. "You. Go."

"I'm not saying he didn't write the song," he said. "It's just that I … *improved* it with my guitar solo. I made the song better. Because of that, I think I deserve song writing credit."

"Is that true?" I asked Guillotine.

Guillotine made a thinking face. "I don't know if I'd say that," he said.

"Yes, you would," Saint Snider said. "We've talked about how much the audience digs that song, especially the solo. It's part of the song now."

"Would the song be the same without the solo?" I asked Guillotine. He gave me a non-committal shrug.

"It wouldn't," Saint Snider said. "It isn't."

I nodded at the two JD's. "What do you guys think?"

They gave me a pretty good copy of Guillotine's non-committal shrug.

"Here's what I think," I told them, "But you guys are

170

gonna have to make up your minds yourselves. I'm not a band member. I can't solve these kinds of problems for you."

Another group nod.

"The song was written by Keith Guillotine," I said. "He *created* it." Both Guillotine and Saint Snider straightened, for exactly the opposite reasons. "But," I continued, "Saint Snider *created* his solo. A solo that now, arguably—based on audience response—has *improved* the song. Become part of it. I mean, can you imagine *Sweet Child O' Mine* without Slash's riff? Of course not. It wouldn't be the same."

"So you're saying that just because he provided a solo riff, he should get co-songwriting credit?" Guillotine asked quietly.

"I'm *not* saying that," I clarified. "I can't say that. Only the four of you can say that. But another word for band is *team*, and if one member of the team provides something that makes everything better for everyone, it would be my opinion that they deserve some recognition for it. You're either in this together or you go out and find solo careers."

Guillotine nodded his head, slowly at first, then faster as things fell into place. "That makes sense," he said. "I guess."

"I never meant to say it wasn't your song," Saint Snider said. "But it was *my* solo."

"Yeah. Yeah, I get that."

"So we all on the same page?" I asked.

Guillotine and Saint Snider nodded again. The two JDs shrugged.

"Do I get songwriting credit for a drum fill?" JD2 asked.

"Don't push it," I told him.

CHAPTER THIRTY-ONE

Marina's smile was full of malevolent delight.

"So you saw them?" she asked me again. "You saw them kiss?"

"Tongue and all," I said. "A quick one, admittedly, but it was not the kind of kiss you'd give a friend or business associate."

"I hope his wife catches the bastard," Marina said, taking a sip of her chardonnay. "And cuts his dick off."

"Whoa! Easy girl!"

"Well, he deserves it."

We were at the bar at Barrelhouse 101. Marina was drinking Chardonnay and I was sipping a Stone IPA. Our server stopped by to let us know our burger was almost ready. Marina thanked her and turned excitedly to me.

"So who do you think she is?" she asked. "That woman?"

"Don't know," I said. "Doesn't matter. I don't think it helps me at all." I tilted my glass in her direction. "But I knew you'd like it."

"Just another reason to hate the bastard," Marina said. "So how *is* the search for Diego's killer going?"

"It's pretty much flat-lined," I told her. "I've learned

basically nothing so far and there are so many different possibilities that I don't know where to begin. Virtually everyone in Ventura County had reason to want Diego Garcia dead. That's a hell of a lot of potential suspects."

Marina sipped her wine. A perfect pink replica of her lips appeared in lipstick on the edge of her glass. "Why even bother?" she asked coldly.

"Because Johnny is a hot head," I told her. "And he would look weak if he let someone kill his brother and get away with it."

"So what's your next step?"

"I'm going to go through that box Andy gave me again," I said. "See if anything jumps out the third time through." I took a sip of the IPA and let its pleasing bitterness wash over my tongue. "After that, I don't know what I'll do."

"You should go see Hankie," Marina suggested.

I nodded. "That's a good idea. I should have thought about that earlier."

She beamed magnificently.

"I'll call him tomorrow and make an appointment," I said. "I need a haircut, anyway."

"Yes, you do," Marina agreed.

We drank silently for a moment. "What if you can't find them?" Marina asked. "What if you can't find out who killed him?"

"That's a very real possibility at this point," I told her. "And Johnny won't be happy about it."

KNIFEPOINT

"What will he do?"

"What *can* he do?"

Our burger arrived along with an extra plate. They had already split it in half for us. Marina took her half, removed the cheese and onion and passed it to me. I peeled the tomato off my side and passed it to her. Romantic bliss.

"He won't try to hurt you, will he?" Marina said.

"That thought may cross his mind," I admitted. "But it would be foolish on his part."

"Because of Puño?"

"Yes," I said. "And because of me."

Marina took a bite of her hamburger and quickly brushed away a drop of juice that oozed out onto her lower lip and chin.

"Let's hope it doesn't come to that," she said around a mouthful.

I bit into my side of the burger and nodded my head in silent agreement.

CHAPTER THIRTY-TWO

Hankie's place was located in a non-descript strip mall in Saticoy—a small town on the east end of Ventura—sandwiched between a breakfast diner named after the nearby freeway (Café 126) and a doughnut shop, famous for its chocolate éclairs and breakfast burritos. The only signage on the window were the white-stenciled words, "Barber Shop" and a cardboard sign with the shop hours posted in black marker (Open Monday through Saturday, 7am-4pm). I knew those hours were only a suggestion because Hankie and his wife loved to travel and it seemed he was there as often as he was not.

The dashboard clock read 7:35am as I pulled the Camaro into the parking lot and chose a space near the front door of the doughnut shop. The scent of freshly made doughnuts floated through the air and made my mouth water. I went inside, waded my way through the usual crowd of regulars drinking coffee and talking loudly about their week and bought a couple of large, glazed doughnuts, telling the cashier to keep the change (a whopping 72 cents). I took my doughnuts and went next door to the barber shop.

The single chair in the shop was open when I pushed

through the door, a string of copper bells hanging there signaling my arrival. Hankie, rinsing some kind of instrument in the sink, turned to me and his face broke into his huge, goofy, lovable smile.

"Brace! How the hell are you! Good to see you!"

I stepped over and gave him a hug, dangling the doughnuts behind his head. "Good to see you, Hankie," I said, stepping back. "I brought doughnuts."

Hankie clapped me on the arm. "I already had breakfast," he told me. "But there's always room for a doughnut!" He opened the bag, removed a doughnut, took a bite, and then waved at the chair. "Sit down," he said, his mouth full. "The usual?"

I nodded. "The usual," I said. "Short, but not military short. And none of that mud crap afterwards."

"It's hair clay," Hankie laughed, setting his doughnut on the counter. He wrapped a warm towel around my neck, and draped a white sheet over me. "It makes your hair stand up. Makes you seem taller."

"I don't see *you* using it," I teased. Hankie was 4' 11" tops, a not unpleasantly round Mexican man with a bubbly personality that made him the perfect barber … or bartender. I had often told him he could be either.

"So, how's Marina?" Hankie asked. He also had the memory of an elephant. He was one of those people who remembered every name, every relationship, every situation that had ever come his way. It worked in his business—there was no bigger social occupation than that of barber—but that's not why he did it. Hankie remembered everything because he genuinely cared. He was the most "people person" person I'd ever met in my life and he was loved by everyone because of it.

It also made him a great source of information if you happened to be a detective.

"She's great," I told him. "Working too much, as usual, but doing well. And how's Lily doing?"

"Doing well," Hankie said. "She's been working too hard for the past couple of weeks, too. But she sold a house a couple of days ago so she's feeling better now."

"Good," I said. "Now maybe she'll take a couple of days off."

"She is," he said. "We are. Going to Laughlin for the weekend in a few days."

"Good for you."

And so it went, catching up with idle chatter, Hankie dancing around me, cutting my hair with scissors and electric shears, as precise and particular as always.

As the family and friends talk faded, I asked, "So, Hankie, what have you heard about the Garcia brothers?"

Hankie was uncharacteristically quiet for a moment. "You mean Johnny and Diego?"

"Yeah," I said. "Those guys. You ever cut their hair?"

"No, no, no," Hankie said. "But I know the guy who does." He laughed. "I mean, who did. I guess Diego don't need haircuts anymore, eh?" He thumped my arm and laughed giddily.

"Heard anything recently?" I asked. "Anything, you know ... juicy?"

Hankie stopped snipping, stepped back and frowned. "I heard that they weren't getting along, the Garcia brothers."

"Over business?"

"Business," Hankie nodded. "And a girl."

I felt my eyebrows go up. Hankie pushed them back down, tilted my head. Snipped.

"You know who?" I asked.

Hankie shook his head. "Don't think I heard a name," he said.

"Elva ring a bell?"

"No. But that doesn't mean that's not the name ... just that I don't remember hearing it."

"Elva's a janitor in Johnny's building," I said. "Had a thing with Diego, or so she says." Hankie shrugged. "And I saw Johnny with another woman at a restaurant. It wasn't his wife and they were, ah ... *close*," I said.

"Maybe that's the one," Hankie said. "Johnny's pretty famous for being a lady's man."

"Is his wife aware of that reputation? Does she know he plays around?"

"She should," Hankie said. "It's not as though he's particularly careful at hiding it. Maybe she doesn't even care as long as the money keeps coming in. Maybe she fools around, too."

"Maybe," I said. "Did you hear anything else about

179

this girl?" I asked. "Were they fighting over her or something?"

Hankie shrugged. "Dunno," he said.

"How seriously were they fighting?" I asked. "You know, to the point that one might want to kill the other?"

"With people like that, who knows?" Hankie said, and I knew he was right.

"I heard there was a contract out on Johnny," I said. "Heard it was Diego who put out the hit."

"Anything's possible," Hankie said, dabbing the back of my neck with some hot shaving cream, its warm suddenness feeling wonderful. "Like I said, with people like that ..." He unfolded a straight razor and went to work. "What's with all the interest in the Garcia brothers?" Hankie asked.

"Johnny hired me to find out who killed his brother," I said.

Hankie stopped, considered. "Well, that doesn't sound like he had anything to do with it then."

"Probably not," I agreed.

Hankie put down the straight razor and wiped the last of the shaving cream off. "You know," he said. "There were a lot of people who would want to see Diego dead."

"I am aware."

"Probably more than wanted to see him alive," Hankie said, thumping my arm again, giving his goofy laugh.

"Yeah," I said. "Not making my job any easier."

Hankie grabbed the white sheet and pulled it off me

with a flourish, like a bullfighter with his cape. He took a hand mirror and angled it so I could see the back of my head in the wall mirror in front of me.

"You're all set!" he said.

I nodded grimly. "I may not who know who killed Diego Garcia," I told him. "But I'll look damn good while I try and find out."

CHAPTER THIRTY-THREE

My office was starting to look like Andy's, with paper scraps of all sizes, shapes and colors scattered across the room. It looked like a tornado with a neatness disorder had just passed through. Forgotten Coke Zero empties stood like hollow sentries guarding a paper ghost town.

I had decided to try and put the madness of the Garcia Brothers into some kind of order, to see if there was any rhyme or reason to be found. First, I tried organizing everything by groups: Stories about Johnny went into one pile, those about Diego in another. Crimes they were actually convicted of in this group, crimes they were only suspected of in another. I sat back and surveyed my work for about an hour. Nothing jumped out and no missing pieces presented themselves. I picked everything up, re-shuffled and started again.

This time I organized everything by location. If a crime occurred in Santa Paula, it went in the Santa Paula pile. If it happened in Ventura, it was filed there. Court hearings were in the Ventura stack where the courthouse was. The few stories about gang wars went into the Oxnard stack because that's where most (but not all) of that action had occurred.

KNIFEPOINT

I walked around the mess and tried to make sense out of anything. It was worse than before and less than zero is considerable.

I could feel the stiffness of frustration starting to put pressure on my brain. I shook my head to chase it off and once again picked up everything and put it back in the box.

Okay, the simple route now. Chronological order. Should have done that in the first place.

The newspapers Andy had provided me with dated all the way back to 1998 when it was assumed that Johnny had taken over the family business after his father died after choking on a chicken bone at the dinner table. I put everything in order by month, date and year starting with the 1998 date and ending with the story about Diego's murder a week or so ago.

I walked among the headlines and bylines and tried hard to find something new. I didn't. The stacks carpeting my office were merely a document of the criminal empire of the Garcia family's history and their ability to skate through it virtually untouched by the law or justice. It was discouraging, disheartening and disgusting. Once again, I cursed myself for ever agreeing to get involved with this.

I took another walk through the wall of shame spread out before me. Most of the stories were about Johnny and his minions but occasionally the name Diego floated up from the pages. Most of the time, it was stupid stuff: drunk and disorderly, speeding tickets, a DUI or two. But sometimes it was more serious: Armed robbery; assault; grand theft. Nothing that ever stuck. Somebody else in Johnny's organization would suddenly step forward and admit guilt or the charges would be dropped due to lack of evidence. I suddenly realized that Johnny must have cared about his brother more deeply than I realized to go to all the fuss it took to keep him out of prison.

I stopped pacing and stared down at a headline proclaiming: BOY, 12, FATALLY STABBED BY INTRUDER. I reached down and picked it up. It was the story that Powell had mentioned the other day at the park. A young boy and his mother had returned home after baseball practice to find an intruder in their home. Before the mother could call for help, the intruder had stabbed her son and fled. The boy died of his injuries before an ambulance could arrive.

The all-too-familiar feeling of helpless rage burned through my body as I read, the leviathan injustice of the situation filling me with impotent anger. I read the story again, focusing on the last line in the article: *A suspect was arrested near the home but was later released.* The word "suspect" was circled in red pen and an arrow pointing to the bottom of the article led to the name "Diego Garcia," underlined twice. Seems like not only Powell thought Diego was the killer.

I glanced at the date on the article. June 3rd. The murder had taken place on June 2nd, almost exactly ten years before. Ten years in which that rat bastard Diego got away with murder, before he finally got what was coming to him.

June 2nd. Today was June 9th. Diego Garcia had been killed seven days ago. *On June 2nd*. The tenth anniversary of the murder of that little boy. I considered that for a moment and then snatched up the phone.

Powell answered his cellphone on the third ring. "Powell," he said simply.

"Hey, Steve, it's Heller," I said.

"What's up, Brace? I'm in the thick of it here."

"Yeah, sorry. Just got a quick question."

"Shoot."

"The family of that boy who was murdered in Montalvo all those years ago. You said they call you every year to follow-up?"

"Yeah, the brother. Wants to know if there's been any progress."

"When's the last time you heard from him?"

"It's been awhile. He usually calls right around the date of the murder. Early June ..." He trailed off. "Now that you mention it, I usually hear from him by now."

"It's still early," I said.

"Yeah, only the ninth. I'm sure he'll be calling soon. He always does." I heard him bark an order to someone and then turn his focus back to me. "Why do you ask?"

"No reason," I said. "Just putting together a timeline."

"All right," Powell said. "If you need anything else ...

goddammit! Get away from there. You're fucking up my crime scene. Hey, Brace, I gotta go."

"Talk to you later."

The line went dead.

I picked up the newspaper story again and re-read a third time, slowly and carefully. The victim's name was Cary Stevenson (*12-year old Cary Stevenson*, I thought bitterly). His parents were Frank and Eliza Stevenson. He had one sibling: an older brother named Eric.

"Yeah, the brother. Wants to know if there's been any progress."

I fell into my desk chair and pulled the keyboard close. Typed "Eric Stevenson, Ventura" into my browser. My pinky stabbed the Enter key and a stream of data appeared on the screen before me. I paged through the first few pages and found nothing pertinent. I added "formerly" to the search string and hit enter again. The number of hits diminished by almost half. I scrolled through the results and found a LinkedIn page halfway down with "Eric Stevenson, Los Angeles." I read the brief bio there and discovered that Eric Stevenson had relocated from Ventura to Los Angeles almost five years ago. Could it be *another* Eric Stevenson from Ventura? Sure, could be. But probably not.

Google. The private detective's best friend.

CHAPTER THIRTY-FOUR

Marina and I decided to make a day out of it.

My personal assistant (Google again), told me that Eric Stevenson was an "account manager" at Enterprise Ice Cream in Los Angeles. I didn't know if that meant he was in a truck selling Fudgsicles to kids on the street or in the office brokering deals with ice cream manufacturers. But Enterprise Ice Cream was located near the garment district so Marina could shop for clothes while I searched for clues.

We started our morning at The Pantry, a nostalgic, diner-styled restaurant owned by former L.A. mayor Richard Riordan. Marina ordered toast and eggs while I stuck with the corned beef hash. Marina gave me a look of disapproval as I shoveled down tablespoons of the greasy, brown meat and potatoes but the savory salty flavor was worth every ounce of her scorn. I refrained from looking down my nose at her rather boring plain white toast and scrambled eggs.

After breakfast, we headed a few blocks south to the world famous Garment District. I had only been there once or twice before and again I didn't see the big deal. It was nothing but row after row of fashion peddlers operating out of what looked like makeshift shops. I was reminded of the street markets in Tijuana or Cabo San Lucas.

Marina, of course, was instantly enthralled, cooing with delight at a lacey blouse hanging on the front of the very first shop she approached. "That's so cute!" she said. "Isn't it?"

I never knew how to answer that question so I just nodded.

According to the Maps app on my iPhone, Enterprise Ice Cream was a six-minute walk from our current location. I gave Marina a quick kiss, told her I'd call her when I was through, and gave an enthusiastic but uninformed thumbs-up to a short pink skirt she unfurled in front of me.

Most of downtown Los Angeles isn't really as filthy as some people seem to think it is, but it certainly is *gritty*. Just ask Dashiell Hammett. The sidewalks were stained with decades of spilled substances (but at least they weren't sticky) and there were a few homeless folks stuffed into abandoned doorways, sleeping off the crushing exhaustion of being alone. Occasionally, the thick smell of urine oozed out of an alleyway, strong enough to make me cover my mouth and nose with the palm of my hand. Otherwise, my walk to Enterprise was quick and unimpeded.

A grinning plywood clown with a brightly painted face and concentric halos surrounding the top of his head—more like the planet Saturn's than that of an angel—greeted me beside a door with the words "Enterprise Ice Cream" painted on it. I tried the knob and it turned freely so inside I went.

A middle-aged woman wearing a faded, rainbow-patterned t-shirt and an equally faded pair of blue jeans sat at a cluttered desk with the phone pressed to her ear. Our eyes met and she held up a single finger: "Just give me a minute" in business office sign language. As she finished her call, apologizing to an apparently irate customer about a late delivery, I surveyed the rest of the office.

The walls were as cluttered as the desk was, with dozens of clippings of ice cream ads and clown photos pinned and stapled there in no particular style or order. I found an ad for It's It, my favorite ice cream sandwich, and smiled. There was a dilapidated gold sofa against one wall that looked as though it would swallow you if you dared to sit on it. Sun-faded magazines, most of them celebrity rags, were splattered across a dark brown table nearby. There was one door to the left of the receptionist and a grimy window on the other side through which I could see a hallway, plain white and surprisingly unadorned.

Alice, the receptionist (whose name I found engraved on a rectangular plate hidden behind an army of tiny plastic clown dolls standing sentinel on the desk), dropped the receiver into the cradle and looked up at me with what appeared to be a genuinely friendly smile below her thick, black-framed glasses. "Hi," she said. "Can I help you?"

"Sure can," I told her. "Is Eric Stevenson available?"

"Should be," Alice answered quickly. "Can I tell him who's calling?"

I realized she meant "calling" in the more archaic sense, a "short visit" rather than a telephone call.

"Arthur Godfrey," I told her. "Ringling Ice Cream out of Portland, Oregon." I stopped there, hoping she'd give me some indication as to whether Eric was a driver or a desk jockey. Alice didn't disappoint.

"Oh, so you sell ice cream, do you?"

I smiled sweetly. "We do."

Alice hunched her shoulders conspiratorially. "Did you bring any samples?" she whispered.

I frowned and shook my head. "Afraid not," I said. "Just wanted to touch base with Eric since I was in the area."

Alice pouted with mock disappointment. "Oh, well," she said. "Let me see if he's got a minute." She pushed away from her desk, stood and waddled through the door on her left into the hall. A moment later, I could hear her voice buzzing in the other room and another, deeper voice burr in reply. Another moment passed and then Alice was back, holding up that "just one minute" finger again.

"He'll be right with you," she said. "Have a seat."

I shot a glance at the hungry sofa along the wall. "That's okay," I said. "I'm sure he won't be long."

Three minutes later, Eric Stevenson walked through the door, a bright smile on his face and his hand extended in greeting. He looked younger than I expected, probably a couple of years shy of 30, and was a few inches taller than I was. He, too, wore faded blue jeans and a black button-up shirt. He also wore the tired, life-worn features of a man who's lived a tough life. Maybe like a man who lost a brother to murder.

"Eric Stevenson," he said. "Glad to meet you."

"The pleasure is mine," I told him. "Arthur Godfrey, Ringling Ice Cream."

"Arthur Godfrey?" Eric asked. "Like the movie star?"

"More of a TV star, really," I said. "But, yes, like that. No relation."

Eric laughed. "Well, come on back," he said, eyeing my empty hands curiously. "And show me what you got."

"Thanks, Alice," I said as we stepped into the hall and headed toward Eric's office. She gave me a playful wink.

Eric led me down the almost eerily undecorated hallway, past a door on the left that led to a utilitarian bathroom and a door on the right that led to a cavernous garage. The third door down was his office.

"Please, sit down," he said, indicating a battered, rather uncomfortable looking metal chair in front of his desk. I smiled my thanks and sat, surprised at how comfortable the chair actually was.

I glanced around the office as Eric took his seat behind the desk. Like the hallway, the walls here were also unadorned and, in fact, the only item that seemed more personal than business was a small photo frame on Eric's desk. Two young girls, probably 4 and 6, beamed out with joy and love from the photo there. *Just the girls*, I observed. *Probably divorced*. Brace Heller, detective at work.

"So what can I do for you, Mr. Godfrey?" Eric asked.

There was no reason to beat around the bush. "I don't want to waste your time, Mr. Stevenson ..."

"Please, call me Eric."

"I don't want to waste your time, Eric, so I'll come straight to the point. I apologize for the ruse, but I'm not an ice cream salesman."

Eric smiled but I was unsure whether it was from uneasiness or suspicion. "I kind of gathered," he said. "You didn't bring a sales kit and, well, you really don't look the type."

"There's a type?" I asked.

"There is," Eric said. "Salesman are pretty much alike the world over, no matter what the industry. And you don't look like a salesman."

I shot a glance at the photo of the girls. "Your daughters?"

"Yes," he said. "Loves of my life. You have kids?"

"Not yet," I told him. "Maybe not ever. Got a dog."

"For some people that's the same thing." A moment of silence passed between us. "So what can I help you with, Mr. Godfrey?"

"Actually, it's Heller," I told him, flipping my card onto the desktop. "Brace Heller. I'm a private detective."

"Oh," Eric said quietly, tugging my card over to the edge of his desk and eyeing it. "From Ventura?"

"Yes."

"Is this about my brother?"

"Actually, it's not," I told him. "It's about somebody else's brother. My client's brother. A man named Diego Garcia."

Eric's demeanor changed in an instant. He transformed from a businessman whose well-manufactured charm brought him continued sales success to a human brick wall built of anger, stand-offishness and defiance. He sat stock still, challenging me to continue.

"I know the name," he said at last. "He's the man who killed my brother."

"He is."

"What about him?"

"He's dead."

I had hoped for a burst of relief, of vengeful satisfaction, of closure. But Eric's expression didn't change at all. Instead, he continued to stare at me with that frozen face.

"So?" he said at last.

"So I thought you'd want to know."

"Yeah, so now I know. Anything else?"

"Actually, yes, there is."

He stared at me through dead eyes. After a moment, his eyebrows raised in question. I took a shot in the dark.

"Can you account for your whereabouts the night of June 2nd?"

Anybody else would have registered shock, horror and anger at that question. *What? You think I'm a suspect?!* Eric's demeanor didn't change at all. He continued to stare at me with a face firm with defiance. After a moment, he said very quietly, "I have a feeling you know where I was."

I nodded. "You were in Santa Paula," I said. "Looking for Diego Garcia."

Now it was Eric's turn to nod. "I was. And I found him. And I put a bullet in that fucker's head. He killed my little brother for no earthly reason and he got away with it for ten years. I gave them ten years to make things right, and they couldn't do it. So I did it myself."

I nodded again.

"And you know what?" Eric continued. "I'm glad I did it. I'd do it again, if I could. I wish I'd had the guts to do it years ago. Not only did he kill my little brother, he might as well have killed my parents, too. They were never the same after that day. Neither was I. Our family was destroyed. And why? Because my brother walked into his own room when that bastard was robbing *our* house." His face twisted darkly in sudden rage. "*He breaks into* our *home and then kills my little brother because they caught him in the act? FUCK that piece of shit thug!"*

I got up silently and closed the door to his office, then returned to my seat. Eric glared at me with an expression that was part rage, part defiance and part daring me to say something.

So I did.

"You don't want the whole world to hear you confess this," I said.

"I don't care *who* knows," Eric said.

"Yes, you do."

"Why? The minute you leave this office, you're going straight to the cops. Everyone's going to know anyway. And I don't give a fuck."

I looked at him calmly across the desk. "Yeah," I said. "About that."

For the first time I saw a completely different emotion in his eyes. It was hesitant, it was cautious, but it was there: Hope.

"Here's the thing," I said. "Diego Garcia was, in fact, a piece of shit thug. And what he did to your brother, and your family, is unforgiveable. And it's not the only heinous thing he did in his lifetime, not by a long shot. So when I found out somebody put a bullet in his head, I was not exactly, let's say, heartbroken."

Eric slowly sank back into his seat and took a deep breath.

"So I'm not particularly inclined to go to the cops," I said. "And if I tell my client that you killed his brother, the cops will be the last thing you need to worry about."

Eric turned his palms up. "Then ... then what are you suggesting?"

"I'm suggesting that we both forget this conversation ever happened," I said. "As long as you give me the gun you used and you swear to never speak of this again."

Eric absorbed that information for a second, then tilted forward and opened the lower right hand drawer in his desk. He pulled out a wooden box, sat it on the desktop and slid it over to me. I tripped the latch and peered inside. Tucked in a bed of red velvet cloth sat a cold gray pistol. A 22 caliber Röhm RG-14, the same kind of gun John Hinckley used in his attempt to kill President Ronald Reagan.

I closed the lid and pulled the box closer to me. "You shot him from the street?" I asked.

Eric nodded.

"Difficult shot to make with a weapon of this type," I said. "Saturday Night Special."

"My dad was a firm believer in the Second Amendment," Eric said. "Took us to the range every week from the time we turned ten. I still go at least once a month."

It made sense. Standing, I tucked the wooden box beneath my arm. "I need you to do one more thing. Call the Ventura Police, ask them how the investigation is going with your brother. You've called every year for the past ten years. If you don't call this year, it will look suspicious. Do the same thing next year, and the year after that. Except for that, you never mention this meeting to anyone again. Ever. We clear?"

Eric nodded. "Yes," he said, and his face crumpled and I could see he was trying hard not to break down and cry.

It seemed like a good time to leave.

"Have a good day, sir!" Alice said brightly as I stepped through the lobby.

"You, too," I told her. "Maybe next time I'll bring samples."

Twenty minutes later, I was standing beside Marina, my arms overflowing with plastic bags full of recently purchased clothing, a wooden box with a murder weapon tucked away inside one of them.

"Did you get what you needed?" she asked me.

"I did."

She gave me a curious look but decided not to pry.

I smiled. "Can we go home now?"

Marina gave me a tired but contented smile. "We can," she said.

And we did.

CHAPTER THIRTY-FIVE

Puño and I sat in my office, quietly contemplating. A box from Bunny's Bitchin' Tacos was on the desk before us. I had just finished a "Fiery Fury" taco and my mouth was buzzing with Habanero spiciness. Painful but delicious.

"So," Puño said around a mouthful of taco, "You're going to let him get away with it."

I nodded. "Got a problem with that?"

"Nope," Puño confirmed. "Just sayin'."

He took a big bite of his taco. Miraculously, despite its messiness, none of it wound up on Puño's black t-shirt.

"So where does that leave you with Caesar?" he said, after chewing for a moment or two. I noticed that his taco didn't leave him with beads of sweat on his brow like mine did.

"Screwed," I said. "I can't tell him I didn't find his brother's killer because he'll never believe it. But if I tell him I did find him, but won't tell him who it is, he'll kill me."

"Or die trying."

"Maybe," I agreed. "I'd rather not deal with all that drama."

"So what are you going to do?"

"Hell, man!" I spat. "Why do you think I asked for this meeting?

Puño held up his hand. "Tacos?" he asked.

"Oh, yeah," I said. "Tacos."

The box on the desktop emptied quickly and soon was sporting only oily stains that nearly made the Bunny's logo illegible. I sipped at my Coke Zero while Puño nursed a Budweiser bottle, which I kept in the mini-fridge just for him.

"So what would *you* do?" I asked Puño.

"Me?" he replied. "I'd go up to Johnny Caesar's house and shoot that fucker in the face."

"Would you have a Plan B, perhaps?"

Puño considered. "I'd tell him I knew who killed his brother but that the guy who did it had a good reason for doing it and that I was gonna let that be."

"And how do you think that would go over?"

"Not good," Puño said. "If I even got out of the room, I'd be looking over my shoulder for a long time. Maybe the rest of my life."

"And that's my dilemma."

"And Marina's dilemma, too," Puño said.

"And yours."

"Yes," Puño said. "Mine, too."

I sat back. My stomach wished there were more tacos, but my waistline was glad there weren't.

"I'm going to give this a few days," I said. "Mull things over."

"Muse," Puño said.

"Yes, *muse*," I agreed. "Maybe a solution will present itself to me."

"Probably not."

"No, probably not." I sighed. The empty box on the desk top stared back at me, its oily stains beckoning. "So," I said to Puño. "You wanna go get more tacos?"

CHAPTER THIRTY-SIX

The afternoon sun was just beginning its smooth decline into the glittering slate blue ocean as I pulled the Camaro into the driveway at home. My shirt pocket vibrated and I pulled out the cell phone slotted there. The number on the phone told me it was Destiny from the Ventura Theater.

"Your boys ready for tonight?" she asked. "They got soundcheck in one hour."

"We'll be there," I said, beaming with confidence. "They're gonna kick ass."

"I'm sure they will," Destiny replied. "See you there."

"You got it."

As soon as Destiny disconnected, I quickly punched in Keith Guillotine's number. He answered on the third ring.

"You guys ready? Soundcheck in an hour."

"Packing up now," Guillotine said.

"I'm going to shower and change and I'll meet you there," I told him.

"Sounds good. Um, hey, Brace ..."

"Yeah?"

"Oh, nevermind. I'll talk to you when I see you."

"Everything okay?"

"Yeah, fine. See you shortly," he said and disconnected. *Great*, I thought, *sounds like more band drama. Better not fuck up the gig tonight.*

The phone rang again. Marina.

"Hey, hot stuff, what's up?" I said.

"You'll pick me up in an hour?" she asked.

"More like half an hour."

"Okay, I'll be ready."

"See you then."

I tapped out of the call and stepped out of the Camaro. The old rock'n'roll excitement rang through my bones. I was managing a band that was opening for Tommy Hogart. Not too shabby. It was going to be a great night.

CHAPTER THIRTY-SEVEN

My eyes didn't want to open, but I peeled back my eyelids anyway. Had to blink about seventy times to clear the gritty sleep out of them.

To my surprise, Marina lay beside me, her chest rising peacefully and hypnotically in deep, relaxed sleep. The morning sun streamed like yellow lasers through the half open blinds but didn't seem to bother her in the least. Wurzel lay beside her, his back tucked flush against her upper thigh.

Lucky dog.

I closed my eyes again and took a deep, satisfied breath. I had been certain that the night before would be one to remember and I hadn't been disappointed. *Weapons Grade Charm* had killed it. Destiny had given them the second opening slot and the theater was nearly full when they took the stage. The crowd hadn't even heard of these guys when they started but, by the time the show was over, the band had them eating out of the palm of their hand. They were brought back for not just one but two encores. And you know you're doing something right when the internationally-known headliner complains to theater management that an opening act was too strong.

The guys were happy because they sold out of merchandise—every last t-shirt and CD—and had cash to celebrate until the wee hours of the morning, which we did at the Sans Souci and, when that closed at 2am, a room at (where else?) the Gila Motel.

My brain felt like it was sitting on a bed of desert sand that coated the walls of my skull as I carefully climbed out of bed and silently got dressed. I think I may have zipped up too loud because suddenly Marina stirred and said "Good morning" from the bed, in a voice thickened with sleep.

"Good morning to you," I said, giving her a soft kiss on the cheek. "I was surprised to see you stayed over."

She smiled sweetly.

"You're still going to make that side of the bed, aren't you?"

She answered me with a sharp slap on the shoulder "What are we doing today?" she asked.

"I've got some research to do down at the office," I told her. "What about you?"

"Got to meet some clients downtown at the Sunrise Hotel," Marina said.

"When will you be done?"

"About noon."

"Wanna meet at the Botanical Garden for a walk?"

"Sure."

KNIFEPOINT

"And then we can go to Cajun Kitchen for lunch."

"Works for me."

I never said no to beignets.

CHAPTER THIRTY-EIGHT

I was sitting in the Camaro, waiting in line at the Chick-fil-A drive-through, when I re-considered my plan for the day. First, I needed a biscuit and a large Coke Zero to undo the damage JagerBombs had done to my stomach the night before. Second, I decided not to go back to the office to pore through the boxes full of Garcia Brothers information that Andy had given me. I'd been through those multiple times and was sure I'd gleaned pretty much all I could glean. I had to find a better use of my time.

I thought about Johnny and the girl he took to lunch the other day—and the fact that she wasn't his wife—and wondered how I could use that.

I paid for my Coke Zero, told the pretty clerk in the window thanks, and winced at her *Stepford Wives*-ish, "My pleasure," response. Doesn't anybody just say "You're welcome," anymore? Then I pulled out of the drive-through, hopped on the 101 North, and peeled off on the 126 toward Santa Paula.

It was much quieter on 10th Street than it was on my previous visit but that was to be expected because today wasn't a work day. I parked the Camaro on the opposite side of the street from The August Building, sipped my Coke Zero, and, as Puño had suggested, *mused*.

Somehow, I had to find a way to tell Johnny Caesar that, yes, I found the shooter who killed his brother and no, I wasn't going to tell him who it was. Caesar wasn't going to like that. If he didn't just shoot me on sight, he would no doubt try to force the name out of me, either by physical torture or via threat of physical harm to my loved ones. That, of course, would be a bad move for everyone involved, for it would be the first wave in a sea of ever-increasing violence until Puño was the last man standing.

And there was no doubt in my mind that Puño would be the last man standing.

I wouldn't say Johnny Caesar was *afraid* of Puño, but he respected him and he knew that Puño would deliver exactly what he promised. Johnny, however, being overcome with emotion—both with the grief of losing his brother and his anger at me for keeping the name to myself—might be blinded to that danger and make a stupid move anyway. The resulting bloodshed wouldn't benefit anyone …

… except, of course, Ritchie the Bean, but he didn't have a horse in this race and he wasn't ambitious enough, or sober enough, to take over his biggest competitor's empire if something happened to Caesar.

The problem was that there was no question that I had to tell Caesar the truth. If I lied and said I failed, his reaction would no doubt lead to violence. If I tried to blame someone else, either someone who deserved to die or someone who was already dead, Caesar would eventually discover the ruse and we'd be back to square one. There was no other path I could think of that would end up with all of us skipping off on our merry, non-intersecting ways.

Shit, maybe Puño was right. Maybe I should just shoot Johnny in the face.

I sat across from Caesar's building and ran scenario after scenario through my mind. None of them ended well. A mild case of despair began to set in as I realized I really only had one shot.

The girl that Johnny was seeing on the side. Who was she? Could I use her as leverage? Threaten Johnny with revealing his affair to the world? Maybe his wife already suspected. Or maybe Hankie was right, maybe she even knew. Maybe they had an arrangement. There was no obvious pat ending. I needed more information and I cursed myself for not at least taking her photo when I followed them to the Inn. I mean, that's why they made cellphones, right? To take pictures?

And what the hell was I doing here now? It was a Saturday, the building was empty. Unless the janitorial staff was here and I could track down Elva, this was a completely wasted trip.

KNIFEPOINT

That mild case of despair grew into something bigger. A moderate case of despair, maybe. I felt as though my back was against the wall and there nowhere else to turn.

I sat there for another hour, finishing my Coke Zero and chewing noisily on the ice, then started the car and headed back to Ventura.

CHAPTER THIRTY-NINE

Keith Guillotine was sitting on the floor in the hallway near my door when I arrived at the office. He looked exhausted, not surprising after the evening he had had, but managed to get to his feet as I approached.

"How you feelin'?" I asked him, as I unlocked the door. "Helluva night. You guys kicked some serious ass."

"Wassup, Brace," Guillotine said. His voice sounded as tired as he looked.

I walked through my tiny waiting room and into my office, tossed my keys on the desk and plopped into my chair. Guillotine stumbled to the visitor chair and fell heavily into it.

"Beer?" I asked, half-joking.

Guillotine made a face. "No, thanks," he said. "I drank enough last night to last me for the rest of week."

I laughed. "You earned it. It's not often the opening act blows the headliner off the stage. I bet we sold more t-shirts than Hogart did."

The hint of a smile flicked across Guillotine's face and then faded. I began to suspect something was eating at him.

KNIFEPOINT

"Okay," I said. "What's wrong? You guys fighting over who wrote what again?"

Guillotine rubbed his hand across his tired, unshaven face. "No, no, it's nothing like that. It's just that ..." He looked down at the ground, as though ashamed, like a kid who's done something wrong and is hesitant to confess it. "It's just that we got an offer last night. A pretty big offer..."

I eyed him cautiously. "Well, that should be *good* news," I said, silently seething that I had been left out of the loop. "Why do you look like somebody kicked your dog?"

"It was a management offer ..."

"You've already got a manager."

"... from Devin Sunshine."

I felt myself stop breathing. "*The* Devin Sunshine?" I asked stupidly.

Guillotine nodded, his eyes still searching the floor.

Devin Sunshine was one of the biggest managers in the rock'n'roll industry. He had made more bands famous than anyone I could think of, and he had developed a public personality that made him as familiar to rock fans as film fans were to Steven Spielberg. He was sort of an idol to me, the kind of man who makes his way in the world doing what he wants to do, what he loves to do. His record was almost unblemished; virtually everything he touched turned to gold.

And now he had touched Weapons Grade Charm.

"So," I said. "Where does that leave me?"

Guillotine was quiet for a moment as he toyed with a stray thread that jutted from the arm of the chair. Finally, he said, "He asked me to talk to you. See if you'd let us out of our contract."

"He can buy me out."

"He won't. He made that clear. He doesn't want to be involved with anybody but the band."

I expected as much. Sunshine didn't get to the top without stepping on a few shoulders. "What are your feelings on this?" I asked.

"I wanna go with him," Guillotine said, finally looking up from the carpet to me. "We *gotta* sign with him. You understand, don't you, Brace? He'll make us *huge!*"

I stared back at the man sitting across from me, fighting back the feelings of betrayal and rage that were burning through me. Weapons Grade Charm was a great band with huge potential and I had seen it. I had scored them the perfect opening gig, a gig they themselves could not score, a gig where they not only delivered perhaps the best performance of their lives but that they did so in front of one of the biggest rock'n'roll managers in the history of the genre. I wished fervently that I had known he was there, that I had spoken to him, pitched the band to him, but I also knew that wouldn't have made any difference. Sunshine was using the band's own goals and dreams to push me out and I knew there was only one way this was going to work for anybody.

212

"I won't get in your way," I said. "Go ahead and sign with Devin Sunshine."

Guillotine looked up at me with what I think was genuine sadness. "Brace, I …"

"Forget it," I told him. "Thank me in the liner notes, or something." I gave him a wan smile; anything brighter would have been impossible.

He returned a smile that was equally as weak and nodded quietly.

"Now get the hell out of here," I told him, failing at an attempt of another smile. "I got work to do."

Guillotine climbed slowly out of the client chair and walked toward the office door. He opened it and turned back. "Thanks, Brace," he said, and walked out.

My elbow dropped to the table and I caught my forehead on my palm. I suddenly felt hollow and useless.

Goddammit. I was so fucking close.

CHAPTER FORTY

Marina knew instantly that something was wrong.

We were walking above the old Ventura Courthouse, where they had built a winding hiking trail through the hills that eventually took you to Grant Park on top, where the famously controversial Serra Cross overlooked the Pacific Ocean. They called it the Ventura Botanical Gardens and, although there was plenty of flora to take in, it was the expansive view that got you. As you faced the ocean, you could see most of downtown Ventura in all its modern retro glory, the Ventura Pier and miles and miles of deep blue sea. It was breathtaking, each and every time we took the walk.

"You're a little down," she said. "After last night I thought you'd be through the roof. Hungover?"

I bristled briefly at the suggestion but pushed it away. "No," I told her. "Just feeling sorry for myself. Everything seems to be going wrong all at once and it's frustrating as hell."

"Like what?"

"Well, for starters, the band fired me."

214

"What?!"

"Keith Guillotine was at the office this morning. Told me they'd signed with someone bigger and better."

"Who?"

"Devin Sunshine."

Marina was quiet for a moment. "Well, he is *bigger*. Not sure about the *better* part. But can they do that? Don't you have a signed agreement with them?"

"I do," I said. "But I'm not going to stop them. Wouldn't be fair to the band. They're not much more than kids. This is their dream. I try to stop them now, with a lawsuit or whatever, and it'll destroy them before they ever get started."

Marina looked at me sadly. "But it's your dream, too."

I nodded slowly. "Maybe," I said.

We walked up a small path that branched off of the main walk. There was a bench made of stone there, and several types of flora planted specifically for informational purposes, like a living museum. Small black signs with white lettering identified each plant and said a little about their history and characteristics. Marina led me to the bench and we sat.

"Well, that sucks," she said. "I'm sorry to hear that. We had such a great time last night."

"It *was* pretty great."

She bit her lip. "I could tell you that you'll find another band, another singer, another artist, but that'll feel pretty empty right now, won't it?"

I nodded.

"So I won't. What else is going on? I'm assuming you haven't found the person who shot Diego Garcia?"

"Actually, I have."

"You ... What? You didn't tell me."

"I was going to, once I figured things out."

"What do you mean?"

"Well, it's not cut and dry," I said. "I found the person who pulled the trigger, but I don't want to tell Johnny Caesar who it is."

"Because he'll kill him?"

"That," I agreed. "But also because his brother deserved to die. He was a piece of shit sociopath who didn't care who he hurt or who he killed and the world is a better place without him." I took a deep breath of the refreshing saline ocean air. "Plus, the guy who killed him had a good reason. A *really* good reason."

"Who was it?"

"It's better you don't know," I said. "And that's another part of the problem. If I tell Caesar I know who did it but I'm not gonna tell him, he may come after you. If I try to bluff him and he finds out otherwise, he may come after you. I don't want him to come after you. First, I'm rather fond of you and second, if anything happened to you, Puño would go all scorched earth policy and I'm not comfortable with all that bloodshed." I gave her a look. "Especially yours."

Marina frowned. But there was more to tell her. "And then, to top things off, Diego's girlfriend came to see me, thinking I could pin his murder on his brother. I can't, of course. He didn't do it. And, if I let the real murderer slide, I'm doing her a disservice. And she seems like a really nice, genuine person."

"Sometimes there is collateral damage," Marina said. "Be thankful it's only emotional."

"I know," I told her. "But I don't have to like it."

"No, you don't." She was quiet for a moment, as she considered all the information I had just given her. Finally, she whispered, "So what are you going to do?"

"I don't know. I'm trying to figure that out."

"And how's that going?"

"Not very well."

Marina stood up from the bench and whipped her leg over my lap, straddling me. She put her forearms on my shoulders and leaned in close. Her silky straight black hair dangled and danced in my face.

"You'll figure it out," she said, kissing my cheek gently. "You always do. And this is why: You've got me to come home to every night, you've got your friends and your family here, you've got Wurzel … and you live in a place that has a view like this …"

She put her palms on my cheeks and turned my head over my left shoulder so I could see the sprawl of downtown Ventura, the crown of the Ventura Theater, the green grass of Mission Park, the spindly brown finger of the Ventura Pier, the sparkling blue ocean that spanned out to the darkening horizon.

After a moment, she turned my face back to hers. "Things may be shitty now but you're still one lucky fucker. It will all get better and you know it." She kissed me gently on the lips. "So snap out of it and get walking or we'll never make it back by lunchtime."

Marina sprang off my lap and headed back down the pathway to the main walk.

I was right behind her.

CHAPTER FORTY-ONE

Lunch at the Cajun Café was delicious, as always, even though Marina chastised me for ordering a patty melt. Apparently, I should have chosen something more Cajun-y. The truth of the matter was that the only things that really mattered were the beignets, which melted in your mouth with doughy, sugary delight and made you believe God loved you.

Marina headed home ("God, I need a shower!") and I went back to the office and gathered up all the Garcia brothers material Andy had loaned me. Too late, I realized I should have brought him a patty melt, too. My showing up with no food was not going to go over well.

Andy was at his desk, as I knew he would be on a Saturday. It was his favorite day to be at the office because there were fewer people there than any other day and he could get more work done. He frowned as I wheeled the file boxes in on the folding dolly I always kept in the car.

"Done with those already?" he asked.

"Yep."

"Help you any?"

"Didn't hurt."

"You bring any grub?" Andy said. "I'm dying here. I need like a cheeseburger or something."

"Um, no," I said. "Sorry. We just had lunch at The Cajun Café."

"Goddammit!" Andy said, without venom. "You should have brought me some beignets."

"I should have. Sorry."

"Freaking lunch room here is a joke," Andy vented. "They've got kale salad in there now. *Kale!* Freaking newsroom with kale salad! Do you think Edward R. Murrow would eat kale? I mean, I'm not asking for much. Maybe just a goddamn Payday!"

"You want me to go grab you something?" I offered. "Carl's Jr is right around the corner."

Andy considered for a moment and then said, "Nah, I'm good. He rocked back in his office chair and put his feet up on the lower drawer. "So nothing in there helped, huh?" He indicated the Garcia brother boxes.

"There was a lot in there that *helped*," I said. "But it was really Google that saved the day."

"Fuckin' Internet," Andy spat. "It's killing us, Brace. Killing us all. Newspapers are gonna be extinct soon."

"Still be online."

"Not the same."

He dropped forward and snatched a manila folder off his desk, tossed it to me, and rocked back in one well-executed motion. "Here's some more stuff I accumulated after you took the boxes," he said. "Check it out before I file it with the rest of it."

I slid the folder over, picked it up and opened it. There was about half an inch of newspaper clippings and printed pages from the web stuffed inside, and I flipped through them casually. The case was solved after all. I knew who did it. I just didn't know what to do about it.

Then I came to a photo near the bottom of the stack and sat forward so violently that the rest of the papers, and the folder, fell to the floor in a jumbled heap.

"Please," I said to Andy. "Please tell me you know who this is."

And I pointed to a photo of Johnny Caesar and the mystery woman I'd followed to the Glen Tavern Inn that afternoon. They were in front of the movie theater on Main Street together, during a food festival or something.

Andy craned his neck and stared through his glasses at the photo I was holding up.

"Yeah, I know who that is," he said. And he told me.

And, suddenly, everything came together.

CHAPTER FORTY-TWO

It was ten o'clock on Monday. The traffic noise outside my window had diminished to post-rush hour standards. I could see a sliver of blue sky through the cracked window in the wall and thought it looked like the kind of day that might burn those clouds off by noon. There was a cool ocean breeze blowing its salt breath through the air.

We were silent as we waited.

Powell sat against the wall in a folding chair. His eyes were hidden by the aviator-style sunglasses he wore and he sat so still that as far as any else could tell he might have been sound asleep. I knew better. He was wide-awake, on-the-alert and ready.

Puño sat on the other side of the room, a familiar sawed-off shotgun propped against the corner beside him. He was finishing a breakfast burrito he'd bought off the food truck that stops downstairs sometimes. He's brave like that.

KNIFEPOINT

I was at my desk, the right hand drawer slightly open, the Sig Sauer in the drawer well within quick, easy reach. Also in easy reach was my other pistol, a Glock 37, which sat on its edge on the floor beside my foot.

It was quiet except for the sound of Puño's mechanical chewing.

Then there was the muffled sound of the elevator doors down the hall, followed by three pairs of shoe soles squeaking on the tile floor. A moment later, the office door opened and one of Johnny Caesar's bodygoons stuck his head in, flashed an expression of mild surprise and distaste at the sight of Puño and Powell, and then stepped back to allow his boss to pass.

Say what you want about Johnny Caesar, you can't say he's stupid. The minute he saw Powell and Puño, his face darkened. He entered the waiting room, hesitated for a split second, and then strode boldly into the office, taking the chair I had centered directly in front of my desk. He shot his eyes to the left at Powell, then to the right at Puño, just to let me know that he was aware they were there … and that they didn't worry him.

"Is there any particular reason," Johnny said with a hiss. "That your friends are here?"

"There is," I said. "We've got a lot to talk about." I nodded my chin at the bodygoons who had taken their usual bookend stations. "You may want to ask your employees to step outside."

"Anything you can say to me, you can say in front of them," Johnny said. "They're just here to make sure I like what I hear."

"That's unfortunate," I said. "Because you're not going to like anything I have to say. And, worse, you're not going to be able to do anything about it."

Johnny's lip wrinkled, revealing his disturbingly perfect teeth. "I guess that means you didn't find out who killed my brother," he said, his lips barely changing from their grimace.

"Actually, I did," I said. "It had more to do with luck than it did with good detective work, but I know who killed Diego."

Out of the corner of my right eye, I saw Powell's hand slowly fall down to his holster and touch the butt of his gun. Otherwise, he hadn't moved.

"Name," Johnny whispered. He sat calmly in the chair, staring at me with eyes that were as cool as a reptile's. But I could see that, like a reptile, he seemed ready to strike.

"Not gonna give you that name, Johnny," I said. "I won't."

Johnny's eye twitched, giving his arched lip some competition in the menacing category. "Name," he said again, in a lower, slower tone.

I shook my head again. "No."

Johnny shifted uneasily in the chair. I could feel his rage heating to the boiling point quicker than I liked.

"Why?" he asked. It came out almost silently, like a whispered hiss.

"Because your brother wasn't a very good person, Johnny," I said. "He was cruel and vicious. And he didn't have your good sense to know when to stop. He made a lot of enemies, and a lot of good people had good reason to see him dead." I paused, took a deep breath. "And the person who killed him had a *very* good reason to do it."

"The fuck is this?" Johnny asked, slamming his hands on the arms of the chair as though he might leap out of it. "I paid you to find the person who killed my brother. *My brother, man!* And I want a name. And I want it *now, goddammit!*"

"You're not getting that name, Johnny," I said. "I know it's hard to hear, but your brother brought this on himself. He finally hurt the wrong person and that person had every right to put him down."

"*Fuck* you," Johnny snapped, and sprang from the chair to his feet. Instantly, his two bodygoons had their guns drawn, their barrels pointed directly at the center of my chest.

Just as instantly, Puño had the sawed-off in his hands and Powell had drawn his service weapon. I looked down to see the Sig Sauer in mine and wondered when I had pulled it out of the drawer.

"You're gonna tell me who killed my little brother, you son of a bitch," Johnny said, his teeth clenched together like Clint Eastwood in a spaghetti western. "Or I swear to God we'll splatter you all over this room."

For a few tense seconds, we all stood still like department store mannequins in a window display from a Quentin Tarantino movie. The air crackled with electric tension.

"You think we won't kill you," Johnny hissed, "just because the cop and the *cholo* are here?"

"That's exactly what I think," I said. "Now sit down. We've got more to talk about." Very slowly, very carefully, I put the Sig Sauer back in the drawer. "This would be the point that you ask your employees to wait outside."

"Yeah?" Johnny growled. "And why the fuck is that?"

"Because I don't think you want them to know about what you've been doing at the Glen Tavern Inn."

Johnny actually jerked, as though someone had shot a quick bolt of electricity through him, and I saw the blood drain from his face.

More concerning, I saw a flash of new raw rage there as well.

"Outside," Johnny said in as low and as menacing a tone as he had used all day. His minions must have caught it because they both lowered their weapons and backed quickly out of the office, through the waiting room and into the hallway.

The door closed behind them.

Puño got up and closed the door to my office as well. Johnny sank slowly back into the chair, like a puppet on strings being gently lowered to the floor. For a few moments, it was quiet.

"So here's how this is going to play out," I said. "I am *not* going to give you the name of the person who killed Diego. I'm sorry, I know it's hard to lose a brother but sometimes turnabout is fair play."

Johnny nodded minutely.

"In return, you are going to do *nothing*. You're going to go about your business like you always do. You can mourn your brother in any way and for as long as you want, but you will not pursue this any further. You will not come after me or any of my friends and family. You will not threaten us in any way. You will not harass or threaten the friends and family of anyone in this room. I won't say you will forget this ever happened because I know it's impossible to forget the death of a brother. But everything else ends here. Now."

Johnny sat back in the chair and took a deep, deep breath. "What if I disagree with your little plan here?" he asked quietly.

"Then we'll tell the world you're *shtupping* your sister," I said, tossing the photograph Andy had given me earlier onto the desk top. Johnny didn't even look at it. "And if anything happens to anyone in this room, or their family or friends, there are at least two others who have this information, and the power to distribute it." I tapped the picture with my forefinger. "The world will know, Johnny. Your business partners, your friends, your family."

"No one will believe you."

"I think they will. But even if they don't, it doesn't matter. Just the possibility of a scandal like that will follow you like a shadow for the rest of your life."

"What if I told you I don't care who knows?"

"I'd say you're full of shit," I said. "This kind of scandal might not destroy your business world, but it'll sure screw it up for a while. And it *will* destroy your family, and it *will* destroy your sister, your mother, your wife, your kids. Is that something you want?"

Johnny looked toward the floor.

"Of course, it isn't," I said. "Let it go, Johnny. You know in your heart that Diego brought this on himself. You had to know that, someday, something like this was going to happen."

It took a few seconds, but Johnny finally looked up at me. He face was drawn and, for the first time since I'd known him, he looked weak. "What if it was your brother, man?"

I tried to look sympathetic but it was impossible for me to think of someone like Diego Garcia as a brother. "I'd be angry," I said, "But I'd try to understand that this was no random shooting. Diego wronged someone who fought back. I don't see how you can hold that against them."

KNIFEPOINT

"Anybody else finds out about this," Johnny said, so softly I could barely hear him. "Everyone in this room is dead."

"Take your best shot," said Puño.

"We'll cross that bridge when we come to it," Powell said quickly, shooting Puño a look.

Johnny sat silently for a moment, his chin on his chest. Finally, he stood slowly—again like a puppet on a string—and straightened his suit. He turned and headed for the office door.

"Do we have a deal?" I called to his back.

"Not much of a deal," he murmured, continuing to the outer office door.

"Do we have an understanding?" I called.

Johnny stopped at the door, his hand on the knob. "Yes," he said simply, and opened the door and walked out.

We were quiet until we heard the elevator doors down the hall open and close again. Then, Powell finally slid his service weapon into its holster. "You trust him?" he asked.

"We didn't give him much choice," I said.

"He'll let it go," Puño said. "He's not stupid. And, criminal or not, his family is a religious bunch. If word got out ... well, it would not be a good thing." But I noticed Puño was still holding on to his shotgun.

"I guess time will tell," Powell said, heading for the hallway. "You gents have a nice day."

The door closed behind him and Puño fell back into his seat, his shotgun straddling his lap. "Think I'll stay awhile," he said casually. "Case somebody shows up needs some shootin'."

CHAPTER FORTY-THREE

It had been a few weeks since I told Johnny he'd never know who killed his brother and things had been okay. When a crime lord promises you he won't kill you or those you love, you still walk around with what feels like a target on your back, everywhere you go, at least for a while.

But, so far, everyone involved was still walking and talking. And that meant no blood had been spilled.

Marina and I walked into O'Leary's with considerably less cheer than usual. It wasn't that we didn't like O'Leary's (we did) and it wasn't that we weren't going to drink (we were). It was that we came with some news that, while not necessarily bad, might have a negative effect on our friend Kristyn.

It almost broke my heart when she looked up from behind the bar, caught sight of Marina and me, and cried out happily, "Hey, Brace! Hey, Marina!"

We took the two seats at the end of the bar, near the junction of the bottom of its "L" shape, as Kristyn spun two compressed paper coasters, each advertising a type of

Lagunitas Brewing beer, onto the bar before us. "What can I getcha?" Kristyn asked.

"Lemondrop, please," Marina said.

"And I'll have a Lagunitas IPA," I told her, nodding at the coaster. She flashed us a big smile and turned to retrieve our drinks, but I caught her hand. "But first, we have to talk," I said. "Can we go into the office?"

"Sure," Kristyn said, her eyes betraying uncertainty and puzzlement. She flipped open the bar flap and stepped into the nearby office. We followed her in and I closed the door behind me.

"Is something wrong?" Kristyn said the moment the door shut.

"It's about Ian Kilgore," I told her.

"Oh, my God!" Her eyes were as wide as saucers. "Is he out?"

"No, sweetie," Marina said gently.

"He's dead," I said, as softly as I could. "They found him hanging in his cell this morning. Used the bedsheets as a noose, apparently."

A tsunami of emotions flashed across Kristyn's face. I could see relief there for a moment, and then puzzlement and finally guilt. She looked up at me with eyes that tried to be defiant, but the confusion was clear behind them. "Well, that's good," she said suddenly, uncertainly. Her shoulders hunched and she scanned the floor blindly as her thoughts came too fast, one after the other. I'd seen it before. Kristyn hated Ian Kilgore more than any other human being in the world but she never wanted him dead. Some people are so good, they mourn the loss of any human life, evil or not.

Me, I was glad the little prick was dead.

In my opinion, Kristyn should have been elated. Her boogie man was dead. He would never bother her again. But Marina had been concerned that Kristyn would be plagued by an unexplainable guilt. She said she'd seen it before in others, in her clients.

I didn't know how much of an effect Kilgore's death would have on Kristyn, but I was glad that both Marina and I were there together when she got the news.

After a few minutes, Kristyn nodded softly. "Okay, thanks guys." She stood and took a deep breath. "I'd better get back to work."

She left us alone in the office. I turned to Marina. "Think she's going to be okay?"

"Probably," she said. "Might be a rough couple of days, but these things fade. Some faster than others."

It was my turn to nod thoughtfully. "Come on," I said. "Don't want our drinks to get warm."

CHAPTER FORTY-FOUR

The day was so bright and sunny that I had turned off all the fluorescent lights in my office and was playing Angry Birds on the iPad. No more boring ass solitaire for me. There were no potential clients in the outer office, the phone sat silently on my desk—content in its useless-ness—and I was already thinking about what to have for lunch. It was 8:30am.

I was mindlessly slinging birds at pigs when the phone decided to do its job and rang, cutting through the saccharine sounds of the video game like a blunt machete. I pushed Angry Birds aside and picked up the receiver, visions of paying customers dancing in my head.

"Heller Investigations."

"Oh, hey, Brace," said a familiar voice. "It's Keith Guillotine."

"Well, I'll be damned," I said. "Mr. Rock Star. How you doin', Keith?"

"I'm good, Brace. Great, actually."

"Good to hear. What the hell are you doing up this time of the morning? Rockers don't even go to bed until after noon."

"Well, it's 11:30 here," Guillotine said. "We're in New York."

"Really?" I replied, feeling a little tightness in my jaw and the first tingle of jealousy as its thin, green fingers reached into my mind. "What's up in the Big Apple?"

"Devin just signed us up for a world tour," Guillotine said. "Next summer, we're opening for Dead Meat."

Dead Meat was one of the biggest heavy metal bands on the planet, one of the few that stuck it out through the 90s and still had a huge fan base today. They were brutal, ugly heavy metal, far too extreme for my tastes. I never would have teamed Weapons Grade Charm up with music of that style. In my opinion, it didn't fit.

Then again, I had never signed *any* band up for a world tour, so what the hell did I know?

"Sounds great," I told him. "They pay you well?"

"Enough," Guillotine said. "We're not going to be buying Maseratis any time soon, but at least now we can say we're professional musicians."

I laughed. "That's more than most can say."

It was quiet for a moment, and then Guillotine said: "Well, I just wanted to call and give you the news. And to say thanks, again. We wouldn't be here without you."

"In more ways than one," I said, laughing to take the edge off.

"I know," Guillotine said. "Really, Brace, I know."

There was another moment of awkward silence. "All right, man," I said. "You guys kick some ass out there.

When you hit L.A., you let me know, okay? I expect front row tickets."

"You'll have them, Brace," Guillotine said. "I promise."

"All right, man, good talkin' to you."

"Good talkin' to you," Guillotine replied.

I dropped the phone back in the cradle and went back to Angry Birds. There, in my modest office, with the phone not ringing, the client room empty and my checkbook getting there fast, playing a stupid videogame. Meanwhile, the band I discovered was going on a world tour with one of the biggest acts in the world.

I decided what I was going to have for lunch. Two big dirty martinis across the street at Café Fiore. Maybe three.

I sat back in my chair and chucked the iPad on the desktop. Even Angry Birds didn't sound like fun anymore. I opened the desk drawer, pulled out the bottle of Makers Mark, and prepared to drink until I no longer felt sorry for myself.

The phone rang again.

"Heller Investigations."

"I feel like pulled pork sliders." Marina.

"Um. Okay."

"So, I'm thinking Ventiki. You can have that spam crap you like."

"It's not crap," I said. "It's called Spamageddon and it's delicious."

KNIFEPOINT

"Whatever."

"Can I have a Mai Tai, too?"

"Sure. Meet you there at 11:30?"

"Perfect. See you there."

"Gotta go. Bye."

I hung up the phone, smiled, and picked up the iPad. Angry Birds squawked at me.

Suddenly, I felt 100% better.

ABOUT THE AUTHOR

R. Scott Bolton lives in Ventura with his wife Shelley, his son Josh and his dogs, Leo, Zoey and Pretzel. He hosts internet radio shows for fun and you can listen to them by visiting his internet radio station/podcast studio at www.RoughEdgeFM.com.

Scott loves to hear from readers and welcomes e-mails at rsb@rscottbolton.com.